# One Last Letter

## PEMA DONYO

# CRIMSON ROMANCE

F+W Media, Inc.

Published by
Crimson Romance
an imprint of F+W Media, Inc.
10151 Carver Road, Suite 200
Blue Ash, OH 45242. U.S.A.
*www.crimsonromance.com*

ISBN 10: 1-4405-8447-8
ISBN 13: 978-1-4405-8447-3
eISBN 10: 1-4405-8448-6
eISBN 13: 978-1-4405-8448-0

*For my amazing sister, Kelsang. You're endlessly supportive and encouraging, whether correcting my horrible sense of direction or responding, "Sure. Write a historical romance."*

# Acknowledgments

Tara—thank you for believing in my book! And a HUGE thank you to my editor, Julie Sturgeon, for the hilarious edits: "Otherwise, we had men dancing with just dresses. Probably not the most graceful dancers they could find."

Thank you Mom, Dad, and all my friends who put up with me suddenly disappearing off the face of Earth to write another chapter.

And, of course, to my readers. This one's for you.

# CHAPTER ONE

*1869*

Dearest Eve,

I hope this letter finds you. I'm praying you write back to this one, Eve, because Lord knows I've been spending way too much time writing to you and not enough time helping your father out. Spelling's improved, though. I can say that much. You taught me well.

Do you remember that, Eve? When the sun was down and I'd sneak out to your front porch and you would meet me there? Back when your dad didn't have that big old guard dog, back when you taught me how to read and write by lantern behind your house?

I hope you remember that. Memories of you are all I seem to have nowadays. I can't ever forget your face, but I'm sure the years have changed it a bit. You could send a picture, you know. My address hasn't changed.

Or you could send a letter. I know you're busy with school and all that, but I'm starting to feel like you've forgotten me.

I'm still back here at Hamilton, Texas. I'm still waiting.

Say something, Eve.

—Jesse

Jesse Greenwood looked up from the paper he was writing on to the blue sky in front of him. *A year.* A whole year since he'd seen her long black hair flying behind her as she raced across the field on the back of a horse, challenging her mount with verbal commands and physical kicks every chance she found. A whole year since she'd made him promise he would keep writing to her while she was away. A year since he'd spoken to her at all.

Maybe she didn't receive his letters. The idea had dawned on him before, especially when he was all by himself out on the ranch. Maybe her father kept the letters from him. Maybe someone at that fancy school of hers burned them before they could reach her hands.

He watched the herd of cattle graze on the pasture. The cattle were lazy, chewing cud all day and staring blankly at any lone cowboy who tried to herd them. They didn't worry about not receiving letters.

One letter out of—how many was it now? Thirty? Forty? Every spare moment he had ended up filled with writing to her. Maybe it was time to give up. He swallowed feelings of surrender. No, he'd promised to write.

Jesse sighed. After putting away the paper, he headed back toward his horse. Promises sure were hard to keep when you didn't know if the other person gave a damn. As he herded the cattle to head back to the ranch, the sun began to set. The fading light filled the sky with deep purple and orange hues. There was no way Eve could see that sunset off on the East Coast, where the sun probably never shined and children probably never learned how to race horses.

"Hey, Greenwood!"

He turned his head at the call of his name. Another one of the ranch hands, Preston, rode up next to him. The beginnings of a beard peppered Preston's jawline, reminding Jesse that he hadn't shaved in days. He didn't really shave anymore, ever. There didn't seem much incentive when Evelyn wasn't around.

As if reading his mind, Preston slapped Jesse's back and whistled low. "Your girl's coming home."

Jesse nearly dropped the folded letter in his hand. He tucked it into his pocket instead and tightened his hands on his reins for a better grip. "What did you just say?"

Preston arched an eyebrow and grinned. "You heard me, all right. Evelyn Lancaster's headed back to Hamilton."

While his eyes never strayed from the cattle he and Preston were taking back to the ranch, Jesse's body was on autopilot. With the trail to the ranch memorized, his mind whirred, trying to process the information Preston had given him.

Preston headed off in the opposite direction and took the cattle from the other side as another ranch hand opened up the gates. Jesse waited until Preston finished trotting around the extent of the corral. Either Preston's daily check of the corral needed more time today, or he was just taunting Jesse. He stepped out of the stirrups and jumped to the ground, his hand drifting to his pocket where the letter lay in the process. When Preston finished, he finally let go of his reins and also dismounted.

The two guided their horses back toward the stable. Jesse could feel Preston's eyes studying his expression. "I ain't lying. She's back for good."

His throat felt dry. "How would you know that?"

Preston chuckled. "Heard it from the big bug himself. 'Make sure Blue Star is ready, Preston.' That was when I asked. Boss said she's come back to be married. Heard she's become real pretty now, too." Preston took off his beige hat as they stepped out of the stable. Once they reached the house, he stamped his feet on the mat in front of the porch door. A plume of dust flew up from the mat in a cloud, a tribute to the day's work on the ranch. He brushed off the dirt from his clothes, taking extra care to appear presentable.

Jesse raised an eyebrow.

Preston shook his head. "Not trying to make myself look good for Evelyn—she's your girl."

Jesse took off his black hat and stepped inside. "Not talking about her, Preston. I know who you're trying to impress." Preston Dean had been chasing Jesse's baby sister for the last year, not that

Jesse approved. He figured Preston's interest in her would fade, the way the rest of his friend's annual infatuations did. Thankfully, Loretta Greenwood hadn't shown any interest in him, and Jesse planned to keep it that way.

"She's not too much younger than Eve was when you two got all lovey-dovey. If I wanted to do the same with your sister, then I—"

Jesse shot his friend a warning look, but Preston smirked. "You just wait and see. Loretta will come around."

The two walked down the hallway of the bunkhouse Mr. Lancaster had provided for his ranch hands. Their heavy footsteps thudded against the wooden flooring. The hallway was empty, and Jesse guessed all the other cowboys were eating at the cookhouse.

Beds lined the back of the bunkhouse, each one stacked a level on top of each other to conserve space. The boss hadn't provided them with much, but a clean bed was all Jesse needed. It had been hard trying to find a job after his parents died; landing a place as a ranch hand had also meant Loretta could work in the kitchen and sleep in the big house, which seemed more than generous to him.

He swallowed hard and pulled the letter from his pocket. The folds seemed to ruin it somehow, and he smoothed the paper with care on the nearest table. So she'd returned to be married. His heart knew who she wanted. She'd told him so; she didn't want to marry anyone else.

His heart beat faster, and he felt perspiration begin to gather in the base of his palms. Her father must have come around after all.

There was a knock at the door from the back entrance. Too early for the other ranch hands to return from supper. Preston nearly darted forward to answer the door, but Jesse shot him a stern look. If it really was Loretta at the door, he certainly didn't want Preston greeting her.

He set his black hat on the table before he walked over to the doorway. What was she thinking? It really wasn't proper for his sister to come to the bunkhouse at this time.

He opened the door. "Loretta, I told you for the last time to stop encouraging Preston into believing that…"

His voice trailed off once his eyes recognized the figure standing on the other side of the doorway. His eyes widened, and he felt his pulse racing.

The girl at the door was definitely not Loretta.

"Hello, Jesse."

• • •

Evelyn Lancaster wanted to run away as fast as possible.

It was a mistake. It was one colossal, gargantuan mistake. Worse than Athens ordering the death of Socrates. Worse than Persephone being kidnapped by Hades. What did she think she was going to do? Seconds ticked by as she found herself unable to say anything more. Her mouth felt dry. What was she supposed to say?

He'd changed, more than she would have ever imagined possible. The boyish frame was filled out, and extra years working on the ranch had defined the muscles in his arms under his coarse brown shirt. He'd even grown taller—past six feet, she guessed. His shoulders were broader, and his cheekbones seemed more pronounced than before. His face carried even more of an aristocratic air, but his body seemed undeniably more masculine.

Yet the expression was the same. Jesse Greenwood's same reticent, admiring expression hadn't changed as he continued to stare at her like she was hand-blown glass. His brown hair still flopped lightly in front of his eyes, causing him to brush it away.

"Hey, Eve."

She winced. She hadn't heard that nickname since she'd left Hamilton, Texas, for the female seminary in Massachusetts. No one at her women's college ever called her Eve. During classes she'd been "Miss Evelyn" and "Miss Lancaster."

She cleared her throat. She'd anticipated the awkwardness but not the simple difficulty in forming words. "I returned home a few hours ago. I thought I should stop by and say hello. Is Preston here? Are any of the other ranch hands here?"

Jesse blinked. He didn't respond for a few seconds. The adoring expression morphed to one of disbelief. "Eve, did you get my letters?"

She bit her lip. "I did." Evelyn resisted the urge to embrace him. Doing so would only make it harder to answer his questions with a lie. Instead, she stood rooted to the spot. She wouldn't move a muscle; there was too much she could regret. "They were nice letters. Thank you. But I burned them."

His eyes became cool steel, all traces of admiration in his eyes melting away. "Burned them? But you…" His jaw was set. "Eve, why didn't you write me back?"

"I was busy." She tore her eyes away from Jesse's searing gaze and tried to look behind his shoulder. The sinking feeling in her chest was surely no more than an echo of the past. She needed to leave before all rationality left her. "Just let all the other ranch hands know I stopped by."

"Stop. Eve, I said stop." Strong hands grabbed both of her shoulders, and she looked up in alarm toward his furrowed brow and confused expression. His voice was so much deeper than she'd remembered. "That's all? You couldn't once respond to me?"

She struggled to push against him, but he held her in place. His tone was rough. It increased in volume, rising with each word that tumbled out of his mouth.

"What about the promise I made to you? When you told me that you wanted to marry—"

"Enough!" Evelyn yanked herself out of his hold and glared. She breathed deeply, as if the extra air would give her the courage she couldn't truly conjure up. "I remember what you are referring to. I did receive your letters. I thank you for them. But I did not respond to you because whatever we had before I left for school…" She gulped. The polite tone of indifference faded. "This has to end."

The reaction was immediate. His features crumpled as she stepped back. His jaw went slack, and she saw his hands at his side ball into fists. He looked like someone had just punched him in the gut. Evelyn's heart broke as she watched him step toward her.

"Neither of us has any money."

"So? We never worried before. We said we'd run away…"

She let out a bitter laugh. "To where? Where would we go?"

"Anywhere. Away from here." He edged closer. "You don't have to listen to your father."

"This has nothing to do with him. This is my choice, not his."

A pause. "I wish you chose a different one."

She wished he wouldn't say anything further. The longer she listened to him, the more her walls of resolve crumbled. Saving the family ranch came before her personal choices.

"You are referring to a conversation from a year ago." She smoothed out her dress, as if wiping away the wrinkles would wipe away the intensity of the conversation. "I may have said certain promises with foolish hope…"

"That wasn't foolish hope, Eve." His voice was guttural. She swallowed when she looked away from her skirt to his clenched fists. The muscles in his forearm tightened as he spoke. "We were in love. We are—"

"Stop. Do not speak of that." She narrowed her eyes at Jesse. How could he be so inconsiderate? "Four years has changed us. It has changed my perspective."

Bitterness marked his tone. "It's given you amnesia, apparently."

*If only.* Evelyn pressed her lips together. Images of kissing him by the light of the moon in the stable, sketches he made of her behind the house, poems she read to him after they had finished racing horses around the ranch when his hours finished. All the memories threatened to overwhelm her, and she swayed slightly.

"Know what I think?"

She bristled, and he didn't wait for her response.

"I think you're scared."

Anger flashed through her. Scared? Never. Practical? Definitely. "I am a realist, not a coward. I am giving up on you, Jesse."

He remained silent. She wanted him to reply, to say something, anything. Any words seemed better than the heavy silence that fell between them instead.

She finally looked up. His eyes met hers with a fierce glare. There was no sadness in his expression, only bitter betrayal. His fists had not unclenched. Evelyn believed that if she reached out, her palms would meet the invisible wall suddenly erected between them.

"We are not possible together, understand?" She struggled to keep her voice even. "I need to marry someone who is more financially secure, Jesse." She stepped back again, away from the barrier between them. "I understand that I told you differently before, but time has passed. It is better for both of us if we just forget…" Her voice lowered. "Forget we ever knew each other at all."

He didn't even slam the door. Jesse shut it with as little sound as possible, the lock barely making a noise as she heard the bolt slide into place.

She bit her lip. *If you didn't tell him now, you would have to tell him later. You did the right thing.* Those unbidden feelings, and her body's instincts, had been so much easier to suppress when she was away from him. Every muscle inside Evelyn wanted to run forward and slam her hands against the wood until he opened up and she jumped back into his arms.

Instead, she turned around and walked back toward her home.

• • •

The next few weeks blurred together in a torrent of tears and indecision. All the eligible young men in the surrounding area had asked her father for a chance to court her. Her father brought up each one at supper, highlighting their fine qualities and numerous bags of cash to their name. He never mentioned it out loud, but his message was clear: The ranch was no longer his priority, but hers as well.

But each suitor seemed so weak. None of them would last a day managing a ranch. Everyone pointed to her father's wealth as a reason for marrying her, and none seemed to show genuine interest in her beyond her physical appearance.

"If you're shaking your head because of all the potential beaus you've rejected, I am not surprised. You're wasting your time trying to choose one from that bunch." Annie Inglewood, her best friend, cast a dismissive gaze in Evelyn's direction. The redhead sat on a wooden bench next to Evelyn's vanity, admiring her own reflection in the mirror. "Have you ever considered that maybe you'll never accept any of the suitors?"

"Bosh! There are at least ten more I have not met yet." Still, she wasn't particularly enthused at the idea of meeting another ten bachelors who were most likely going to be as unappealing as the last six. "I could accept one of them."

"None of them is Jesse."

Evelyn drew in a quick intake of breath. "I need someone with more financial stability."

"Then what's wrong with the ones you've rejected?"

What was wrong, indeed? A sinking feeling settled in her stomach. "Or I could pursue a career of my own."

"I doubt Jesse would ever stop you from doing something you wanted."

Jesse this, Jesse that. When would she stop hearing his name everywhere she went in Hamilton?

Annie rolled her eyes and spun around, fixing Evelyn a critical eye. "Why are you so insistent on being married now, anyway?"

"The ranch can use all the financial support it can get." She shifted her weight on the bed, realizing the contradiction between her words and behavior. Then why couldn't she just tie herself to one of the rich fellows who expressed interest?

"Have a word with your father. I'm sure he'd listen if you just asked him for more time."

Maybe Annie did have a point. Jesse could be out of the question, but maybe her father would postpone her marriage and her list of suitors for a few years. There was no time like the present to find out. Evelyn opened the door and walked down the hallway, toward the study. Annie called out her name, but Evelyn ignored her.

She stepped inside her father's room. On one side of the study, the wall was lined with several rows of bookshelves containing dusty tomes ranging in topics from finance to law to agriculture. The sturdy spinning globe she loved so much as a child still rested on a small table in the center of the room. And behind the large oak desk, where papers determining the future of her family's ranch were strewn, sat her father.

Thomas Lancaster set down the papers in his hand when he saw her enter the room. Rarely worn glasses perched on the bridge of his nose. His forehead was creased with worry, yet he smiled when he saw his eldest. "Evelyn, what is it?"

"Father, the list of suitors…" She mustered up enough courage to step forward. Her father's large oak desk seemed imposing, but infinitely more intimidating was her father's expectant expression. "I think we need to talk about who I want to marry."

"Well, of course, go ahead." He gestured his hand outward.

She paused. "I have been giving some consideration to my marriage and I—"

Before she could finish, Mr. Lancaster held his palm up to Evelyn to quiet her for a moment. His gaze shifted to a point behind her. "Come right in, Greenwood."

She stood perfectly still as heavy footsteps approached her father's desk. She had to remind herself to breathe as she sneaked a look out of the corner of her eye at the tall man standing next to her.

Jesse Greenwood's expression was firm, the hard lines of his face even more stern than she'd ever seen them. He smelled of fresh morning air, dust from the trails, and a familiar musky scent that was uniquely his. Her body longed to turn her head toward him and bury her face in his shirt and wrap her arms around him—

No, that was in the past now.

He nodded to her father. "Just wanted to say goodbye, sir, before I hit the road."

Her father smiled at Jesse. Or rather, she knew, he smiled at the lack of interaction he saw between Jesse and Evelyn. "I wish you the best of luck in California, boy. Whenever you want to return to Texas, my ranch is always willing to hire a hand with your skills."

Her eyes widened, but she didn't dare look at Jesse. Surely there was some mistake. He couldn't really leave. Her stomach plummeted.

He just couldn't.

"Loretta's staying, though. She's happy here. I'll send money to her soon as I get settled out West." He placed his hat on his head and adjusted the rucksack over his shoulder. "Much thanks for the horse you provided me, sir."

"It's the least I can do for your years of service, Greenwood. Best of luck on your journey."

She scowled. More like the least he could do to show his appreciation that Jesse was leaving his ranch.

Jesse nodded again, and then turned to leave. He didn't even glance in her direction. It was as if she was invisible to him now.

She heard his footsteps leave the room, felt the air shift as his familiar scent faded, and wanted nothing more than to run after him as fast as she could.

Instead, she stayed still.

# CHAPTER TWO

*1876*

"I'm never going to find love again!" The redhead wailed into Evelyn's shoulder, great sobs wracking her chest and fat tears staining her dress. The tear stains had practically formed a new print on one of the cotton shirtsleeves of Evelyn's dress.

She patted Annie's head and frowned. This was the third time her friend cried over Edward this week. "You must be positive, Annie. Just because he did not want to settle down does not mean every other man is the same."

"There are no other men in Hamilton I want! I only want him! He's the only one for me!" Another fresh wail caused Evelyn to sigh. Annie's behavior was ridiculous, even for her. Edward Beaumont was the town flirt. Everyone gossiped about how he flirted with dozens of girls at a time. How he'd managed to make Annie fall for him, Evelyn would never know.

"You will be fine. Be rational."

Annie shook her head. "You don't understand. He kept telling me he would ask my father to court me. He promised!"

"I do not doubt it. But Hamilton is not the entire world." Evelyn lifted her friend's head from Evelyn's shoulder and wiped away one of Annie's tears. "Dallas is nearby. You have an aunt in the city, right? Live there for a few months. Meet other men."

"But you know I cannot go on my own." Annie shuddered. "Just think of the city filth I would have to deal with. And whose pragmatism will save me from other Edwards? Only you!"

"You are right on that account."

"Exactly! You must come with me."

Evelyn nearly snorted. As if she could protect Annie from falling for every man who showed her a smile. She stood up from her friend's bed and walked toward the doorway.

Annie rushed forward. She put both of her arms on either side of the door frame, blocking Evelyn's exit from the room. "Why will you not come with me? We can find husbands together."

Husband-hunting? She shook her head. Not even if doing so came with ten free horses. "You know my place is at the ranch. I need to help my father every day. I cannot simply leave for a few weeks."

"What are the other cowboys for?" Annie rolled her eyes. Her tears dried at the sudden change of topic, and despair morphed into dismissal. "If we are ever to find husbands, we cannot waste our lives away at a ranch."

"Breighton is my family's ranch, not yours. You do not need to worry yourself about it." Evelyn ducked underneath Annie's arm and headed toward the front door. She heard Annie's footsteps trail after her, but not before Evelyn had already managed to step outside into the fresh Texas air.

The mid-morning bustle of the burg distracted her from meddling musings of marriage. The large general store across from Annie's home buzzed with activity as nomadic traders and roaming cowboys came by to pick up supplies. Tattle-tale town residents delighted in discussions of local gossip outside the doors of the post office, sharing secrets over letters that had traveled farther than they ever would. It was too early in the day for the saloon to be active, but still a few locals brushed in and out of the establishment's doors with a whiskey-influenced walk.

"Breighton is practically my home, too, you know—I spend so much time there." Annie glanced toward the seamstress shop next to her house. "Mother knows I'll eventually take over her dress shop, which doesn't exactly thrill me. I'll grow into a spinster before then!"

Evelyn started toward her horse, her boots clipping against the small pebbles outside of the Inglewoods' home and shop. "Twenty-two is hardly a spinster. You are even younger than I, Annie. You have time to be married still."

She hitched herself onto her horse. "Besides," she said over her shoulder. "There are more important matters for me to worry about than marriage."

Annie sounded incredulous. "What could possibly be more important than marriage?"

Evelyn shook her head as she rode away, beyond the outskirts of the town of Hamilton and toward the ranch of Breighton. The farther she traveled along the long dirt road, the more the fences fell away from the sides of the path and the more open the land became. Of course, nearly all the green pasture belonged to someone. Only the grassy abandoned acres gave the appearance of being still wild and unclaimed.

Eventually she recognized the land as her own. She could see the ranch hands watching over the cattle in the distant pastures. The tall red barn grew more visible as she drew farther up the trail. The sun began to set, that beautiful Texas sunset whose fading red rays hit the plains of her father's ranch as far as the eye could see.

*This.* This was more important than marriage.

She couldn't sell Breighton. Her eventual husband's money would pay off the ranch's expenses. *But where was the husband?* Maybe she was too picky.

She bit her lower lip. No use wondering about "maybes." She couldn't afford to waste time thinking about marriage.

She spurred the horse forward as she raced toward home. The wind whipped through her hair as she leaned toward the horse, closing the distance between them to increase her speed. When they passed the first corral post, Evelyn pulled on the reins, drawing her horse into a trot. The road widened as the narrow trail gave way to a large clearing in front of the stables.

Blue Star trotted to a halt as she approached the clearing. Evelyn grabbed the saddle horn and jumped off, still holding the reins as she guided Blue Star toward one of the waiting ranch hands outside the stables.

"Thanks, Denny. Do you know where my father is?"

"Last I saw, Mr. Lancaster was repairing the fences with the others, ma'am." Denny pointed to the corral where Preston and the other ranch hands were hauling logs near the far end of the fence. She frowned when she noticed her father working with them. What was he doing there? He was in no shape to be doing ranch work.

She walked over to join them. The doctor had already told her father to take it easy until he felt well again. She pulled up the long sleeves of her dress as she approached the men. "I can help, Father. Just let me handle this for you."

"Get back into the house, Evelyn." Her father set the hammer down and cleared his throat before standing. Drawing up to his full height, he stood a good half a foot taller than her. "This is no woman's work. This is—"

Another set of wracking coughs gripped her father. He clenched his fist and held it toward his ribs, beating against his chest as he gasped for breath through the wheezing. She brought herself underneath her father's arm to support his weight as he leaned against her. What was he thinking?

"The doctor told you to rest! You are in no condition to work right now. And we already talked about this." Evelyn pursed her lips together. She wished her father would stop insisting she didn't belong working on the ranch. "This ranch is mine as well. I want to help."

"No, no, no…" Her father finally stopped coughing. He brought her arm down and clucked his tongue. "Someday, you'll be married and the ranch will be his to take care of."

The other ranch hands from behind them stopped working to hear the conversation. Her father turned around and scowled. "What? She's never going to marry any of you. Get back to work, boys!" Her father waved at the ranch hands to continue fixing the fences. He walked away from the fence, bringing one hand behind Evelyn to guide her away from the repairs. "I know you worry for my health, but I'm as fit as ever."

As if on cue, her father's coughs began anew. This time, however, they didn't stop. He sounded like he was gasping for breath as they increased in frequency. Evelyn watched him clap his hands to his knees, unable to stand upright.

"Preston!" Evelyn called out, supporting her father's weight once again. "Help me get him back to the house."

Preston rushed over from the fence and took her father's other side. His coughs continued, wracking his chest with more intensity with each passing second as they practically pulled him toward the house. When they reached the porch, a maid rushed out to take him indoors.

Evelyn opened the door for the maid as she brought him inside. Evelyn's heart hammered in her chest. Her father's illness was even worse than she imagined. "Set him down on his bed and watch over him. Make sure he stays in bed for a while."

Preston folded his arms and leaned against one of the porch columns. "He's in mighty bad shape. Doctor needs to see him."

"I know." She sat down into the nearest wooden chair to rub her temples with the pads of her fingers, hoping the desperate practice would alleviate the building headache. "I plan to go down to Hamilton now and fetch for Dr. Elton myself."

Fetch for Dr. Elton, pay the ranch hands, review the orders for the new inventory—just another task she needed to complete.

And another added expense. She cringed. Not that there was a shortage of those these days. Her father had to fire two of the ranch hands recently for trying to steal from the big house. She had debated whether or not to re-hire after the incident, but pickings were slim. There was a shortage of cowboys in Hamilton. Everyone had heard of a wealthier ranch up north, and most of the cowboys decided to try their luck for higher wages.

There was no way her father could afford to compete with those wages. She sighed. Too bad cowboys didn't work for free.

Breighton had already been operating at a loss for the past few months. The loans her father planned to pay back months ago were still only partially paid. The loan re-payments had to be met, but Evelyn had no idea where the money was supposed to come from. She swallowed hard. Should she start selling the items in the house?

She turned her palms up in her lap. Even the insides of her hands were chapped. Rough calluses framed palms that had once been as smooth as polished stone. Fingers that had only turned book pages now repaired fences and grew coarse from gripping the horse reins. The white buckskin gloves hadn't helped much; blisters still formed daily.

She looked up from her hands and removed thoughts of hardship from her mind. Moping in misery held no place in her life. There was no time to feel sorry for herself, really. With a shortage of ranch hands and the ranch operating at a loss and her father ill—she furrowed her brow. She would have just to work harder.

Nothing she couldn't handle. There was work to be done.

• • •

Jesse wiped the towel across the side of his face, removing the remnants of trimmed hair from the side of his beard. He raised an eyebrow at the reflection he saw in the mirror. Was that him? He rubbed his hand along the length of his trimmed beard.

After reaching into his wallet, he set the cash down on the counter for the barber and lifted himself from the chair to leave. The floorboards creaked underneath his weight as he pushed open the doors and stepped out into the sunlight.

A low whistle caught his attention, and he turned to the source.

A busty young woman with liquor on her breath leaned forward. He held out his arms to steady her, and then set her against the wall. Sheila Danforth. He sighed. Still frequenting the bar and off on another bender, as always. "Too early in the day for liquor, ma'am."

She giggled while she pressed her back against the wooden slats of the barbershop to get a better look at him. In her drunken haze, she kept sliding off the wall and straightening herself up again. Satisfied with her inspection, she started to wobble toward him. "All the better for seein' you, doll. Who are you?"

Jesse stepped back. He'd known her since they were kids. "Don't you recognize me?"

"Don't reckon so. I'd remember that sweet face and body anywhere, baby." Sheila winked, but stopped stumbling toward him. She placed a hand on her hip and rested her weight on one leg, jutting the other straight out in front of her. "You're new around here, aren't you?"

He turned away, shaking his head. She didn't recognize him at all.

As he walked down the row of stores, he grew suddenly aware of the fine fabric of his coat and the sturdiness of his black boots. There was no reason for Sheila to recognize him as the same Jesse Greenwood who left town. His hand brushed against the trimmed beard around his mouth, and he adjusted his new hat. Jesse the cowboy could have never afforded such fine fixings; these clothes belonged to the new Mr. Greenwood.

A small smile crossed his features. He may have changed, but Hamilton sure hadn't.

All the sights and sounds and smells were the same as he remembered. No new inventions had touched Hamilton as far as he could see. The town stayed frozen in time while the world changed around it. He heard the sound of the blacksmith around the corner, the clang of the hammer hitting the hot metal echoing around the bend. In front of him was the general store.

The store looked the same as always, and the apothecary right by it still had the same dusty sign that hung by only one hinge. A red sign reading Doctor perched over the building next to the apothecary. He crossed the trail and headed in that direction, wondering if even the door would look the same as he remembered.

Yep, still that same faded mustard color. The kind that reminded him of sunrises witnessed on horseback and dirt roads. His throat tightened. Working on a ranch nearly felt like another lifetime ago. He hadn't forgotten all the skills he'd learned: herding cattle, mending corral posts. Yet his time at Breighton seemed more like a story someone told him rather than a reality he actually remembered living.

"Is that… no, it couldn't be!" A short, skinny man in his mid-50s approached him. Dr. Elton shook his finger at Jesse, slapped his hands together, and laughed suddenly—out of joy or disbelief, Jesse couldn't say. "Greenwood, is that you?"

He brushed out the sleeves of his coat, suddenly self-conscious. No one in Hamilton had ever seen him in clothes this expensive before. The new fabrics felt like a fancy cloak he hid behind. "Yes, sir, it is. How are you, doctor?"

"Oh my goodness! It's been so long, boy. Well, you're not a boy anymore." Dr. Elton clapped a hand over his chest. He adjusted his spectacles with the other hand. Jesse felt his eyes look him and up down, scrutinizing him like he would a new patient. "You look like a man now, and in a much better position than when you left. What have you been doing all these years, anyhow?"

"I was in California."

"What could you be doing there?"

"Worked at a hotel for a few years until the owner died, leaving it to me. I run the hotel now, me and a few others. Made enough money to be able to travel back here." More than enough, actually. Enough for Loretta to quit her job, enough for him to buy a house for her, and enough for him to pay for her wedding. Enough to buy his own ranch, if he desired.

"Seems like you've done well for yourself." Dr. Elton nodded. He pushed his glasses back up, the inspection over. "What brings you back to Hamilton?"

"Loretta's marriage. I want to see for myself that my sister's settled and happy here before I return to California."

"You won't take her back with you?"

"She wants to stay." Jesse shrugged. She'd begged him to stay in Texas, too. "I'm only here for a few months."

"Have you been to Breighton recently? I am sure they all miss you over there. You and the Lancaster girl were always such good friends…"

Jesse stiffened. It was in the past now, he reminded himself. Lord, how he'd reminded himself. Loretta had written to him that Evelyn wasn't married yet, but it didn't change anything for him. He wasn't enough for her. Never would be. He cleared his throat, about to respond, when the doctor suddenly stepped past him.

"Why, that's her coming up now. She seems in quite a hurry."

Jesse turned around to look at what the doctor was staring at. As soon as he did, he wished more than anything that he hadn't.

The wind whipped her hair behind her, the dark locks flowing in the air. She didn't bother to ride sidesaddle. Her legs rested on both sides of the horse, and she leaned forward against her mount with the reins gripped tightly in her hand. She rode like a cowboy. Jesse had only ever seen one girl ride a horse so fearlessly: Eve.

*Evelyn*, he reminded himself. *She's Evelyn now and you don't care for her.*

Eve—*Evelyn*—didn't notice him at first. Her horse slowed to a trot and she remained seated as she addressed the doctor. "My father needs help," she gasped. Panic seeped into her voice. "I raced here as fast as I could. I know you treated him recently, but now he seems worse. I have no idea what could be wrong with him."

"Mr. Lancaster's in trouble?"

Evelyn looked over at the sound of his voice. She seemed taken aback at first, perhaps doubting her sense of hearing. But when her gaze met Jesse's, her jaw went slack. Eyes wide, she tried to say something, then immediately clamped her mouth shut. There was no mistake that she recognized him. She would say something to him, surely.

He stifled the disappointment washing over him as her gaze passed from him to Dr. Elton.

Her voice became firm once more, as if she'd already forgotten he was there. "How soon do you think you can ride up to Breighton?"

"Well, I'll get my horse now. Mr. Greenwood, I'm terribly sorry we couldn't catch up properly. Next time, definitely. You must eat supper with my wife and me." The doctor shook Jesse's hand, forcing Jesse to tear his gaze away from Evelyn. He nodded to the doctor, promising they'd speak again.

A clopping of hooves drew his eyes back to where she had been. This time, though, there was only a cloud of dust and a distant image of Blue Star riding away from the town. Through all his time in California, he hadn't met a girl who could race a horse faster than his Eve.

Evelyn, he corrected himself. She wasn't his Eve anymore.

# CHAPTER THREE

Jesse Greenwood was back.

Evelyn finished braiding her hair and swept it into a bun. A few black locks protested, hanging to the sides and away from the up-do. She pinned the rebellious strands in place and checked the back in the mirror before rising from her vanity bench.

Jesse Greenwood was back.

The big house seemed so much emptier than she'd ever remembered. Her childhood memories of Breighton included maids buzzing about the house, filling the rooms with idle chatter. But now they were gone, leaving only idle silence. Not to mention her father being confined to bed rest. She crossed her arms and pressed them close to her chest. Sometimes she felt like she was living in the big house all by herself. She missed the maids; she missed company. It was up to Evelyn to manage some of the kitchen chores, but it wasn't too bad. The loneliness was worse.

Jesse Greenwood was back.

She shut her eyes, as if closing them tightly enough could bid away the thought. Turning her attention to the laundry didn't seem to do much good. While her father was bedridden, there was even more she could do to help out. He'd always clucked about her not stooping to household chores like cooking and cleaning. Or riding horses, for that matter.

Jesse had been the one to teach her that skill, not her father. She still remembered the sight of her father being livid when she first refused to ride sidesaddle. Evelyn gave a small smile. Soon enough she was the one to beat Jesse in racing.

How did every thought come back to him? She pulled out the laundry tub and brought it outside to where the maid, Irene, waited with piles of clothes. After checking to see she had enough soap to scrub away the grime, Evelyn walked back into the house to her father's study.

Too bad thinking about Jesse didn't increase the revenue for the ranch. She had just finished the recent calculation of Breighton's profits, or lack thereof, really. She didn't have the heart to tell her father while he was ill. What if learning about the financial burdens made him worse? But the loan still needed to be repaid, and the next payment was due in a week. There was no choice.

She picked up the receipt from the bank. It was possible to find paid work, but she was needed at the ranch as well. So how was she supposed to come up with that amount of money?

"Ma'am?" Irene knocked on the open door. "Jesse Greenwood is here to see you. He's still out on the porch right now."

Evelyn nearly dropped the paper in her hand. What could he be doing here? "Tell him to wait in the parlor. I will be right out."

Irene nodded and left to relay the message.

Evelyn tried not to imagine all the worst-case scenarios for him to see her, but somehow she couldn't manage to brush them away. The possibilities flashed through her mind: he was engaged; he was already married; he was here to insult her for letting him go.

The train of thought stopped the moment she saw his silhouette against the window. He stood in the center of the parlor, his hands clutching the rim of his black hat as he looked around the room. The lace curtains framing the parlor windows served as a backdrop to outline his tall, broad frame.

The years he'd spent away from Hamilton had changed him more than when she'd reunited with him after her time at the seminary. He'd even grown facial hair, for goodness's sake! His jaw had been smooth as a baby's when he was sixteen. Of course, it somehow made him look more attractive. She gulped. Nothing about him looked like the lanky teenage boy who'd left seven years ago.

She bit her lip. Not that he would consider her as a romantic interest anymore. Not after she'd spurned him. The moment Jesse's eyes landed on her, she felt her knees nearly buckle. When had his gaze suddenly turned so intense?

"Ma'am." He nodded to her. Not Eve. Not anymore. She was just another woman to him now. "Can I speak to your father?"

"He is asleep right now." She threw her shoulders back and feigned confidence. While her father was ill, she was the head of the ranch. "You can say whatever you need to me."

He tensed his shoulders. "I come to you with a business proposition."

"What kind of business proposal do you have in mind?" She clutched the bills tighter in her hand. His clothes looked just as expensive as her father's. His coat was tailored and fitted, and his cheeks no longer sported the weathered look hers did. However he had spent the past few years, they'd been kind to him.

"I own a hotel in California. As a result, I have some money that I wish to invest with. It shall accrue much more interest in a project, as opposed to sitting in a bank."

She held her breath. Even his language sounded more gentrified. "You wish to invest in Breighton?"

"I noticed some of the other ranch hands have been let go. Preston told me the ranch was operating at a loss." He shrugged. "I know Breighton. This ranch bounces back from financial trouble better than any other venture. Seems like as good of an investment as any."

She drew much needed confidence from his reminder. Breighton had run into trouble in the past, but her family had always made up for it and made a profit at the end of the day. It was nice to hear someone else finally share the same sentiment.

But the tension remained. She couldn't shake the suspicion tugging at the corner of her mind. Evelyn shifted her weight, unsure of how much to reveal.

"Preston told you the truth. The ranch has fallen into financial trouble. I have not had the heart to tell my father yet. There are…" She hesitated. If Jesse was considering investing in Breighton, who was she to refuse the much-needed help? He deserved to know if he was really considering an investment in the ranch. "There are certain bank loans that need repaying."

"If I were to repay them, I would expect a certain cut in the profits." His stare was stern. His hotel experience had apparently given him business sense. Yet while his voice sounded severe, there was still the same sincerity about him she remembered. Too bad she couldn't trust his sincerity toward her. "The details can be negotiated later. But I expect to be a partner in the ranch with your father."

She wanted nothing more than to accept his offer right away. The ranch would bounce back eventually, she knew. But until then, the bank loans weren't going to pay themselves.

"I will let him know when he's in better health." She could hardly believe her ears. All the nights she'd stayed up, worrying that the bank would seize the land, all the time she'd spent considering the different ways to allocate funds to eke out more revenue—and here Jesse showed up, answering all her prayers.

Maybe.

"Thank you so much. Your investment will help Breighton more than you can imagine."

He nodded, but there was no smile on his face. The invisible barrier between them had never been torn down, she knew. His offer was simply a financial proposal, not an offer of friendship.

"Mind if I take a look around the place? It's been a while."

"Oh, of course. I will show you around." Evelyn opened the front door for him. They headed toward the fences in silence, the clear blue sky above them. She still couldn't believe he was willing to help finance the ranch; a huge boulder had just been rolled off her chest. "The fences need repair. I help Preston and the other boys with that."

Jesse flashed a small smile, and Evelyn's heart lifted. Maybe he was offering his friendship after all. "You help out around the ranch?"

"There is a shortage of ranch hands right now. Some of the cowboys moved up north." They walked past the chicken coops and headed into the barn. They strode down the aisle of horses. The mares and mustangs peered at him through the open stable doors, studying the new arrival.

"Loretta told me about that."

She guided him around the corner to the cows in the barn. Jesse ran his hand along the faded red of the milking stall walls. "I don't just want to invest in this ranch. I want to help out again as a ranch hand."

What fresh torture was this? There was no way she could afford to hire someone else until the ranch started making a profit again. "Oh, but there is no need. Your investment is more than I can ask for."

"No, I want to. I miss working in this place, as crazy as it sounds." He turned from the stall walls to look out at the green pastures in the distance. Barbed wire fences kept the cattle from leaving as the ranch hands watched over them. "Can't quite turn your back on it. Not a lot of green pasture out there in California."

"I cannot pay you." Her voice was urgent and her embarrassment complete, but there was no story she could offer him other than the truth. "While we need help, there are just not enough funds to keep this ranch going at the same pace you remember."

"I'll be working to protect my investment, not for your payment." Jesse put his hat back on and gave her a warning look. "If I'm partnering with your father to get this ranch back on track, I intend to see my profit at the end of this deal."

"Of course." She nearly breathed a sigh of relief. Jesse Greenwood's visit was as surprising as it was welcome. He was only looking for a business deal while he was in town, and he'd chosen Breighton. "How long are you staying in Hamilton?"

"Three months, maybe. Until Loretta's married." He rubbed his chin, his smooth hands scratching over his new beard. The look would take some getting used to, but it fit him. "Encouraged a marriage between her and a doctor's son, Robert. It's a good match."

Evelyn raised an eyebrow. Loretta and Robert? She'd seen Jesse's sister coming around the ranch every week to visit Preston. "But she and Preston have always made eyes at each other. Everyone in Hamilton knows that."

He scoffed. "Ain't no way in hell she's marrying Preston. He's just a cowhand. I'm going to see her into a higher station in life."

She furrowed her brow. "A higher station?"

"She thinks she's in love, but someday she'll understand." His voice was nonchalant. It wasn't cold, exactly, but dismissive.

"She and Preston are inseparable, though."

"Maybe it's better if they just forget they ever knew each other."

Evelyn drew in a sharp breath. There wasn't a day that went by that she didn't remember those last words.

• • •

Loretta ran her fingers over the wooden posts of the corral. "I'm so glad you're helping to fix up the ranch."

Jesse surveyed Breighton's livestock. Glancing over the number of cattle grazing in the far fields was enough to estimate the number of cattle had increased, too. More men were needed to manage such a large herd. "I'm a business partner this time, not just another ranch hand."

"How's Evelyn?"

Jesse shot Loretta a quick look.

His sister rolled her eyes. Her fingers stopped over the top of one of the posts, and she leaned forward against it. "Oh, don't lie to me. You still care for her."

He folded his arms over his chest. "I'm just here for business."

"There's nothing wrong with admitting you care for her." Loretta smoothed out the creases of her lavender wool dress. "You never stopped."

"I never told you that."

"No, you didn't." Loretta stepped away from the corral. She shifted her blond curls to one side of her head, all the while peering at him with a critical eye. "Your questions about her spoke loudly enough. 'Is she married?' 'How many men court her?' 'Does she ever talk about me?'"

He gritted his teeth. "Nothing wrong with trying to keep up with the news in Hamilton."

"You don't care about anything that happens in Hamilton." She smirked. "You came here to see her."

He scuffed his dusty stovetop boots against the dirt. "I barely see her around the ranch anyhow."

"Only because I'm sure you're avoiding her. Didn't she give you a room in the big house?" Loretta asked. She tucked a wisp of blond hair behind her ear, but her gaze wasn't on him. Instead, she stared at the ranch hands behind him. "You're dying to get back out there on the ranch again, aren't you?"

He looked over his shoulder to see what captured her attention, or rather *who* captured it. He frowned when he realized who stared back at her. "Maybe I am. And you're dying to talk to Preston again, aren't you?"

Loretta averted her eyes. She dropped the lock of blond hair she'd been curling around her finger as a pink blush bloomed in her cheeks. "And maybe I am, too."

"He's just a ranch hand, Loretta." Jesse tried to keep his voice even. "I've given you enough money to rise out of that station. Robert wants to marry you. He's from a good family. It's a much better match."

She huffed and walked away toward the house. He turned around to glare at Preston and then followed her. "Loretta! Loretta, come back here."

"No!" She spun around. He winced when he noticed her scowl. "You've already told me who to marry, haven't you? I know I can't marry Preston. But you don't get to tell me anything else. You can't stop me from visiting him."

Jesse stood there as she stormed away. His sister stopped in the clearing in front of the house, where her buggy was waiting. The driver held his hand out for her, but she refused the help and climbed in herself. Without another look at Jesse, she said something to the driver and the horse and buggy began moving down the road toward Hamilton.

"You don't have to be so hard on her, you know."

He turned around at the voice, distracting him from the sound of the buggy wheels rolling away. The voice was soft, feminine, and dangerous.

The sleeves of her oversized blue shirt were rolled up and she wore a pair of cotton trousers underneath. A black-brimmed hat covered her head, and her hair was tucked in a neat bun in the back. Dust covered her clothes. If not for her slim shoulders and short height, Evelyn was just another cowboy helping out at the ranch.

"Seems like she's spirited enough even when I try to scold her." Jesse rubbed the back of his neck. What was he going to do with his baby sister? He hadn't even told her he was working at the ranch again; she'd shown up on her own. Clearly she hadn't been here to visit him. He didn't even want to consider what she would have told Preston if he hadn't been here.

"Loretta is scared of disobeying you." He couldn't miss the fact they were less than a foot apart. He shifted in place as her honeysuckle scent filled his nostrils. "She does not need to be reminded."

"Reminded about what?"

"That she has no choice in who she will marry."

"And if I let her choose?" His eyes glanced at her bee-stung lips, full and slightly parted. They'd chapped from days on the ranch, but they still looked as kissable as he remembered. "She'll choose Preston."

"What is wrong with her choice?"

"He's beneath her."

Evelyn didn't respond. She stared back at Jesse, her lips pressed together into a thin line. "A marriage is something she has to live with for the rest of her life. She should be able to choose whom she spends her valuable time with. She deserves better."

He felt like someone had socked him in the stomach. Was that why she hadn't married him, or anyone, for that matter? No man had been worth her time. He didn't doubt she'd find a husband soon—some rich fella to snap her up with his blue-blooded "better."

"Preston's not enough for her."

"No. She deserves to live a life with love." She lifted her chin upward. "She does not have to live with regret."

He grimaced. As if Evelyn could tell him how to take care of his sister. "She'll understand when she's older."

"She will not." Her voice trembled, which made him question her meaning, though she looked at him with stubborn resolve in her eyes. "She will never understand why she could not marry the one she loved."

"Didn't stop you," Jesse muttered under his breath.

"Excuse me?"

"I said it didn't stop you." He narrowed his eyes. How could she suddenly vouch for Loretta? "Your father never liked me. You listened to him, just like my sister listens to me."

"This has nothing to do with me. Loretta and I are different people."

He suppressed the urge to groan. Her shoulders were still thrown back with an appearance of authority, but her eyes no longer seemed so sure of her words.

"Preston is just a cowboy. Loretta deserves better. So did you."

"Preston could make something out of himself. He could go west, like you did. Then he would be enough for Loretta." The words tumbled out of Evelyn's mouth, as if she couldn't get them out fast enough. "You would let her marry him then, surely?"

Jesse was starting to wonder whether they were talking about his sister or Evelyn. "I may have wealth, but I'm still just a ranch hand at heart. So is Preston. Let's face it—we wouldn't work even if I became king of England. It's about where I come from, not what I'm doing."

Her voice was quiet. "How would you know?"

"Nothing I do will change the fact that my parents abandoned my sister and me, and nothing Preston can do will change the fact that he's an orphan. We don't come from the right families, Evelyn. If the doctor's son wants to marry my sister, this is her only chance at a better life."

"A life devoid of love is not a better life."

He threw his hands into the air. "You don't get it, do you?" He gritted his teeth. "Marriage is the only way Loretta can make it into a better class, a better group of people. Her sons and daughters will all come from the right family. You rich folks just don't understand. You wouldn't know any different."

Anger flared in her emerald eyes and she edged two steps toward him, pointing her index finger at his chest. "I am not some sheltered, upper-class princess, Jesse. I have put more work into Breighton than anyone else here to keep it from going bankrupt!"

He remained silent. She was close enough that if he just tilted his head, his lips would brush past hers. She stood there against him, breathing heavily. The seconds ticked by. Honeysuckle overwhelmed him. Her cheeks flushed and the heat pressed against both of their bodies; her gaze relaxed more and more the longer they locked eyes. Was her heart thumping as loudly as his?

"Jesse!" one of the other ranch hands called to the cowboy. The man's horse neighed and pawed the air for a few seconds. "We need your help. The herd's heading the wrong way!"

Both Jesse and Evelyn stepped back as if they'd been caught doing what was real in his imagination. He cleared his throat, and nodded to the ranch hand. "I'll be right there." He walked away without another glance in her direction.

Years ago, he'd believed nothing was more dangerous than a solitary journey to California. He was wrong.

Resisting the fall back into Eve Lancaster's arms would be the most perilous task of all.

• • •

The years hadn't changed his ability to take her breath away.

There was something about watching him work that excited her, had ever since he'd arrived at her father's ranch with his eight-year-old sister. Her father told her some boy had approached the house himself, asking for a job and explaining that his parents were dead. Eleven-year-old Evelyn thought it was awfully bold of him. She imagined him to be a masculine thirty, unspeakably rugged, and possess a wary look in his eye that had seen the world.

When she actually saw him in person, she was disappointed. He was short, skinny, and twelve. He was all awkward angles and tufts of brown hair, too-long-for-his-body scrawny arms, and a reticent disposition. But then she'd watched him work.

He proved to be their best rider and cattle herder by the age of fourteen and started leading the other ranch hands before fifteen. When the cowboys trotted out with cattle, his horse would always be the one guiding the others. Most times he would sit calmly and poised in his saddle, as Evelyn imagined a king would sit in his throne.

Then when the ranch hands gathered the herd back into the corral, he would lean forward, clucking his tongue and yelling out commands. His shoulders would be thrown back, the lean, corded muscles in his forearms prominent as he rolled up his dusty sleeves. He looked so at ease; he looked at home. There was nowhere he belonged more than on the ranch.

The years hadn't changed him. Not really. His clothes were better quality, and the facial scruff was new, but otherwise he looked just as natural on horseback as he always did. Still the same proud stance with his shoulders back, broad chest puffed out as he commanded the herd of cattle, like not a day had passed since he left Breighton.

If she just stared at him long enough, she could pretend the years of separation had never occurred. She was still that same fifteen-year-old girl holding a torch for her cowboy, admiring him through the window.

It was only when he looked up on his way to the corral now that he noticed Evelyn. She turned her head away from the glass window, cheeks flushed. This was what, the third time he'd caught her staring at him?

She groaned inwardly. That wasn't even counting their encounter after Loretta left. She'd been so angry at him for pigeonholing her with the title of rich folks. She didn't think the rich folks he referred to developed calluses and blisters from working all day under the sun.

Half of her anger had clouded over when she realized how close she stood to him. His mouth had been so close to hers. Evelyn's fingertips brushed her lips at the memory. Just a foolish desire, hoping he would have kissed her. Why kiss the girl who caused you to hightail it all the way to California?

All she'd imagined at sixteen was meeting someone wealthy and supporting her father's ranch. Pursue a career of her own, maybe, which would still be possible by a rich man taking care of the ranch. Jesse didn't have a penny to his name back then. Her stomach twisted. Funny how things changed.

How could she have been so foolish? She wasn't even Anne Elliot from *Persuasion*. At least the main character had been persuaded by a mentor; Evelyn had made the decision by herself. She swallowed hard. But she had been so sure she was making the right decision. It was the *rational* decision.

Evelyn looked down again at the stack of financial documents in her hand. Thinking about him could wait. The papers couldn't. She strolled into her father's bedroom.

He was still lying down, but his eyes were open and focused when he heard someone enter the room. "Evelyn? Come closer." He beckoned her to sit down, but his voice still sounded feeble. "Doctor tells me I'm slowly getting better."

"Just rest, Father. The ranch is in good hands." She pursed her lips. "I made this month's payment to the bank. Jesse's contribution has certainly helped."

Her father nodded. Mr. Lancaster hadn't been in a position to refuse his help either. All she had to do was show him the numbers and he'd nearly started another coughing fit until she informed him Jesse was willing to pay back the rest of the loans.

Her father sighed. "Not excited at the idea of sharing profits with a former ranch hand, but Breighton must be saved."

"He is not just a ranch hand, Father." His words echoed in her mind. Her father was wrong; he needed to already recognize him as more than a cowboy. "Jesse is your business partner right now."

"For now, that is." He waved his hand to dismiss the topic. "How are the cowboys taking the wage cuts? No serious complaints, I hope?"

"About the wages, Father… the cuts may not be enough. Another ranch hand has to go. I calculated the numbers, and if we want to start operating at a profit within the next two months, those wages are going to have go back into investing in the ranch. Jesse's technically working for free, so he can cover the extra work." She handed the documents to him. Her father gazed out the window, where the ranch hands were taking out the cattle to graze on the pastures.

"I've got to get better soon and head out there to work with the boys."

"No, you have to rest here. Working out there is only going to prolong your illness."

"What illness? I'm as fit as a fiddle!" As if to prove a point, Mr. Lancaster attempted to sit up, and promptly began wheezing. Evelyn laid him back down again. He settled back against the pillow with a frown on his face.

"I told you not to worry about the ranch. I am already helping out."

"But you're wasting such a good education. You said you would be a doctor, a lawyer…"

"They were dreams, Father." Her heart ached at the reminder. The ranch had fallen into financial trouble so quickly after she'd decided to continue studying at an academy. A decision didn't always lead to a future. Further education was out of the question once her father admitted he couldn't run Breighton alone. But she'd made the choice to stay. "Breighton is my home, too. I care about this place just as much as you do. Now rest. The documents are here for you to read when you feel well enough."

She took the materials from his hand and placed them on the nightstand. Evelyn smoothed out the bottom of her blue dress she'd worn for today. She only wore it these days when she was going into town or seeing her father. Dresses had no place in a corral.

But as long as she was wearing an outfit that didn't shock the townsfolk, she might as well run some errands. The ranch needed more horseshoes, and the blacksmith wasn't going to come to her. She passed through the doorway of her father's room and headed toward her own. After grabbing the payment for the blacksmith and stuffing it into her reticule, she passed by the water basin next to her bed. Vanity got the better of her. She stepped back, crouched down, and took one last look at her reflection.

She'd tried her best not to let ranch life make her let go of her appearance, but long days on horseback hadn't done anything to smooth her weathered skin or keep her darkened complexion fair. Her suntanned, chapped skin looked nearly nothing like the girl who'd returned from an East Coast female seminary. Evelyn smiled at the water's image. No, but her face looked better than she ever imagined it could. It spoke of hard work.

She moved down the hallway, her small boots clipping against the polished wooden flooring. Swinging open the porch door, she adjusted her reticule again. Right as she stepped through the doorway, her shoulder slammed into someone.

Jesse stood in the doorway, coming from the porch side. He turned to his right to get past her, just as she turned to her left to get past him and they ran into each other again. His familiar scent filled her senses and caused every inch of her skin to feel on fire. Her heart raced against her ribcage, hyper aware of his presence.

For a second, he locked his eyes with hers. Did he think about the past as much she did? She suppressed the questions, the many words left unsaid still lodged in her throat.

He finally brushed past her, his shoulder barely grazing hers. She swallowed as his scent swept by her. He'd barely acknowledged her presence each time they saw each other around the house. It was harder to sleep at night knowing he was only a few doors down, with an unlocked door and years of history between them.

Not that she hadn't tried to speak to him. He rebuffed her every time, just like he'd done at the door. The more he drew away, the more she was determined to speak to him about their past. She wasn't just falling for Jesse; she was stumbling toward him.

Evelyn had nearly reached the end of the porch when an envelope caught her eye. The missive was tucked just between two posts that held up the porch, the bright white paper contrasting with the dark wooden slats of the floorboards and the light blue tones of the porch columns. Her name was written on the outside of the envelope.

She rubbed her eyes. Surely she was seeing things. Who would leave an envelope on her porch? But when her vision cleared, the envelope remained. She kneeled down to pick it up. After tearing open the seal, she lifted out the note.

Dearest love,

I see you and all I can think is, "What would we be like together?" Every time your glance crosses mine, my heart can't help but hope that there could be a future for us. You don't seem to mind me, though. Give me a sign. Give a man hope.

Could it be him? Her heart dared to wish. The letter wasn't signed, but the words sounded like his. The penmanship was harried, as if the words were written in a hurry. Maybe this was his way of admitting his feelings for her. She tucked the note back into the envelope and placed it in her pocket. If the letter really was from Jesse, she would be sure to write back.

"Miss Evelyn Lancaster."

The voice from above caught her attention. John Cooper's low drawl called to her from atop his horse. He had an annoying habit of remaining on his mount, as if trying to make the person he was addressing feel smaller. Or to prevent his prized boots from touching dirt. She lifted her hand to shield her eyes against the sun's rays.

"What brings you here, John?" Evelyn placed her hands on her hips and squinted at the judge's son. This was nearly the fifteenth time he'd come by this month.

"Just passing through the neighborhood, that's all." John inspected his nails and then looked back at Evelyn. "Thought I might see how you're getting along since the last time we talked."

She managed a tight smile for his sake. "We just spoke two days ago. And Breighton's a bit out of the way from Hamilton. You cannot really 'pass by it' without meaning to."

John threw back his shoulders, his glossy hair catching the light. He was handsome. If she hadn't already known, Annie would have reminded her till the sun didn't shine anymore. She gushed about him as all the girls in Breighton did, gossiping about his family wealth and his eloquent words. His cropped black hair and fair skin made him look as close as she had ever seen to a white knight. Riding a horse and wearing boots without a speck of dust only seemed to complete the image.

Evelyn, however, had never been one for fairytales.

"My offer to court you still stands, Miss Lancaster." John looked around the farm, his hand brushing past the pistol she knew he had tucked away beneath his coat. "I can protect you from anyone who tries to harm you, I'm sure of it. I am a crack shot with a pistol, you must know."

Oh, she knew. She knew after the fiftieth time he told her; she didn't need to know again. "I appreciate your offer, Mr. Cooper. But my current answer is still no."

"I beg you to reconsider."

"I am always reconsidering." He came by so often that some of the ranch hands probably believed he *was* courting her. She sighed. "You know I welcome your presence as a friend any time you want. But I am in no mind to marry right now."

John sighed. His hand fell from where his pistol lay, ending his play of bravery. The show was over.

"Evelyn, I have no cruel intentions. You know that as plain as anyone. My father likes you. Your father likes me. What, I ask with all due respect, is the problem?"

She had wondered the same question herself. The answer was probably the same as all the other reasons she'd rejected every suitor. Over the years, all the suitors learned to take no for an answer. But not John. He seemed to double his persistence when the others backed out. There was nothing particularly wrong with John, but there was nothing right with him either. He was just another man to her.

"I appreciate you coming by, I really do. Would you like to come inside for a bit?" She gestured to the porch door out of politeness, all the while hoping he'd decline her offer. "Irene made some lemonade this morning."

"No, I think I am fine out here. Remember my offer, Miss Lancaster." He grinned at her, flashing the winning smile that sent so many feminine hearts in Hamilton racing. Just not her own. "I shall be back again."

She couldn't help but breathe a sigh of relief as she watched his horse ride away. She and John had gotten along great as acquaintances who knew each other from church—up until he'd decided he wanted to pursue her as a wife. Her attention turned back to the envelope in her pocket. She scanned over it again, each line echoing inside her head as she read it in Jesse's voice. After the second read, she opened the porch door and went back inside the house.

Once she'd reached her room, she pulled out a small scrap of paper from inside her reticule. Evelyn set the purse down, grabbed a nearby pen, and sat behind the oak desk. She paused after she had spread the note onto the table, unfolding the paper's creases.

Where would she even start? There was so much she wanted to tell Jesse. Whether or not the letters really came from him, she would have an outlet to express her feelings. If she'd been unable to tell him in the past about how his disappearance to California had affected her, she would be able to tell him now. She dipped her pen into the inkwell and began to write.

Every thought she ever wanted to communicate to him in person, all the regrets she faced after turning him down, she vented in the letter. The emotions she bottled inside her released in a sudden flood of words, rushing out to be expressed through pen and paper.

The blacksmith could wait for a few hours. She had a letter to reply to.

# CHAPTER FOUR

Supper was Jesse's favorite and least favorite time of the day.

As a new, though temporary, partner at his ranch, Mr. Lancaster insisted that if Jesse was going to live in the big house, he would eat there, too. Jesse refused at first, but Evelyn told him Mr. Lancaster had taken one look at the amount of money Jesse decided to invest in Breighton and wouldn't take no for an answer. Besides, he didn't have a reason for the refusal. The food inside the house tasted much better than what the ranch hands had.

Afternoon meals were easy enough—whatever the cook made, he'd take in a knapsack and eat on the trail with the other ranch hands. But supper couldn't be avoided. Mr. Lancaster still wasn't well enough to leave his bed, so Jesse took his spot at the table.

While the other men ate in the bunkhouse, he dined alone with Evelyn.

The first few dinners had been, at best, awkward, and at worst, terrifying. The last meal he'd shared with her was before she left for the seminary. Instead of picnics ending with promises and steamy lip-locking sessions, now meals were just thick silence and distant memories hanging above their heads.

Yet their old friendship couldn't stay hidden forever. It took a few weeks for him to no longer go out of his way to avoid her around the ranch, and she to no longer let their conversations lapse into silence. They both had the ranch to talk about, and that topic of discussion brought ease back into their encounters.

"Does Denny slack off? I keep reminding him to put fresh hay in the barn, and he never does. Yesterday he refused to milk the cows until I threatened him." Evelyn regularly asked him how the ranch workers were responding to certain duties or changes in wages.

"He just wants to get out to herding the cattle with the other cowboys, that's all," Jesse replied. "I'll keep an eye on him for you."

"Thank you." Evelyn glanced down at her plate. She pushed the carrots and peas to one side of her ceramic plate, and then back to the other side. "I worry that they are not listening to me now that my father is ill. Do they even see me as their boss?"

"They do." He was always amazed when she admitted her insecurities to him as head of the ranch. Strange, how a woman who seemed so confident could possess so much doubt. "I think they have more trouble listening to me."

"Why would they? They have every reason to listen to you. You are a partner in this ranch now."

"I don't want them to know. I've got no more to my name than the rest of them."

"Now, that is not true." Evelyn shook her head. "You have managed a hotel, you are an investor in this ranch—"

"Still just a ranch hand. Once a cowboy, always a cowboy." He threaded his fingers through his hair. "Wouldn't make a lick of difference to them."

She pressed her lips together and furrowed her brow. Jesse couldn't stand seeing her so worried, especially over him. *She has enough stress already.*

He cleared his throat. "How are the bank payments coming along?"

She beamed. After setting her fork down, she placed both hands on the edge of the table. "Almost paid back, thanks to you."

Fried chicken and buttermilk biscuits lay forgotten after one glance at Evelyn. There she sat, brazenly wearing trousers like a man, yet she'd tucked one slim leg behind the other like a lady. He smirked.

"What is it?"

"Some things are still so ladylike about you, even while you're sitting there wearing britches." He pointed to the evidence.

She shrugged. "Dresses do not hold up well when repairing barns and feeding pigs."

"I'd reckon not." Jesse tried not to grin further. "I'd like to see that, you trying to do the day's chores in a dress."

"Is that a challenge, Mr. Greenwood?" Evelyn lifted her chin in that cute way of hers, showing off the expanse of creamy skin along her neck. "I have done so before, you know. I doubt you could do the same."

"I've never seen another woman wearing trousers."

"Sounds like you are avoiding the question. Would you or would you not be able to?" Her full lips curved upward, strawberry-red lips waiting to be kissed.

He swallowed hard and went back to work on his peas. Green peas didn't taunt him with a glimpse of what he'd never have, unlike Evelyn. "'Course I could." His tone came out gruffer than intended.

She didn't seem to notice, though, and leaned only closer toward him. "I sure would like to see you try." He glanced over at her and blinked as her breasts pushed against the starched material of her shirt. The top buttons of the cotton shirt were undone, and her curves teased him. "I bet you three days of ranch chores that you could not."

"And what do you lose if I win the bet?" Suddenly he wished he hadn't asked that. She just seemed to lean further, naïve to how the fabric constrained her bosom. He tried to look away. But the soft flesh called out to him, preventing his eyes from averting.

"You decide." She laughed, a melodic sound that reminded him of running streams and chirping birds. "I have full faith you can come up with a punishment much more creative than mine."

Jesse stood up suddenly. "Think I'll get back to work now."

"Now?"

"Why not?"

Evelyn looked out the window. The dark dusk showed no cowboys along the horizon. She sounded confused, even startled. "Why would you work now? Everything has been done for today. The sun is nearly down."

"All the better, then. Need to test how some of the horses react to the new horseshoes." He ignored her sound of protest as he headed toward the stables.

The girl was going to get the better of him. Evelyn Lancaster didn't seem to know her effect on him, and he doubted she ever would. The only way he could manage to express himself didn't involve a conversation. Fear gathered in the pit of his stomach. One wrong move and she'd send him packing from the ranch all over again.

As he neared the first stall, he could see Preston talking to a girl who was leaning against one of the walls, Preston's arm on one side of her. He looked at first like he was pinning her against her will, but the girl was laughing at something he'd said. Funny, Jesse was pretty sure he recognized that girl—blonde, tall, and—

"Loretta!" He stormed to the side of the barn. After drawing to a halt before the frightened couple, he gritted his teeth. His sister would never stop disobeying him.

His sister's head turned at the sound of his voice. Her eyes widened and she ducked behind Preston before Jesse reached them. Preston shielded Loretta behind his body, meeting Jesse's glare with a challenging look.

"Let my sister go." His voice could cut steel. "She's engaged to someone else."

"She don't want to be! You're forcing her to do something she doesn't want." Preston scowled at Jesse. "You know she wants to be with me. She wouldn't be here right now if it weren't true."

"It is true! I love him, Jesse." Loretta called out from behind Preston's shoulder and then hid behind him again. Preston's chest puffed out at Loretta's affirmation, as if someone just declared him governor of Texas.

He groaned. "Come out this instant."

"You're just jealous," she said. Her voice shook, and he thought he heard her sniffling through tears. "This is just because of Evelyn."

He set his jaw. "That's enough."

"Just because you couldn't be with the girl you loved doesn't mean I can't be with the man I love."

"I said that's *enough*."

Even Preston seemed to know his girl had gone too far. His wide-eyed glance drifted from the girl behind him to her brother in front. "Hey, baby, you don't need to bring that up now."

"No, Preston, I will." Loretta stepped into view, wiping away the tears streaming down her cheeks. "You're taking out your past on me. Just because you're unhappy at losing love in your life doesn't mean I have to be."

"I said, *that's enough, Loretta!*" His booming shout echoed through the night air. The sound rolled through the far-reaching pastures below them. The setting sun caused darkness to creep over Jesse's heart as well as his vision. "You are never to speak to Preston again, you hear me? Tonight is the last time you are ever going to see him. Preston, take her back to her house. If you're not back here in fifteen minutes, I'm taking her with me to California."

Preston nodded and hurried the sobbing girl away from her brother.

Jesse winced at the sound of her tears. Why couldn't she see his way? He rubbed a hand over his chin, his fingers grazing the stubble he'd forgotten to shave that morning. His shoulders slumped. He just wanted her to have the best life possible.

His sister's words echoed inside his head. He wasn't taking out his situation on her. But Preston would never amount to anything more than a cowboy in his life. Didn't Loretta want more for herself than being the wife of a ranch hand?

• • •

After dinner, Evelyn hurried back to her room and opened one of her drawers. Inside were the letters. After the first one, the author told her he would leave the letters in a tree knothole by her house. Dutifully, she checked the spot daily for the newest missive. The letters were exchanged daily, sometimes with her putting a letter in the knothole in the morning and already finding one in the evening.

Evelyn's fingers traced over the ends of her desk. She lifted each letter out from the drawer, her fingertips brushing over the writing of the latest letter.

Dearest love,

It's harder and harder every day to ignore my feelings for you. I want nothing more than to admit how I feel to you, but you make it difficult for me to express myself without fear of rejection. I shut my eyes and all I can think of is your beautiful green ones, challenging me with that fierce jade gaze of yours, your playful laugh as you find the most random pieces of conversation hilarious, and the hard work etched on the weathered planes of your face. I'd do anything to take away some of that work from you.

The words sent a thrill up her spine. She didn't just love the romance behind each letter; she loved the honesty. There was something sincere about each note. Unlike all the other suitors she'd had, this one actually admired her personality.

Evelyn pulled out a pen and a scrap of paper.

To the unnamed,

I wish you would tell me who you really are. I admit I have certain suspicions, but I cannot be sure. You asked me to give you a sign of hope, to show at least a sign that there may be a future between us. If you may be the person I dare hope, I have tried to extend as much friendship as I possibly can. What else can I do? I admire you from afar as well. Perhaps we have known each other for so long that we have no idea how to start afresh for ourselves.

Second chances are easier wished for than granted. Maybe, though, there is no need to run from the past. We can embrace what happened together, and deal with the future together as well.

Evelyn pulled open her drawer and removed a small envelope. After placing the note inside, she sealed the letter and headed toward the tree. The fireplace in the parlor cast a soft glow over the house and through the hallway.

The porch was dark, and shadows fell across the wooden slats as she approached the steps. One of the ranch hands had left a lantern on the table next to the oak rocker. After placing the envelope in the familiar knothole, Evelyn picked up the lantern on the porch.

There was another light from inside the stables, too. She could make out the long shadow of a man standing in one of the barn aisles. She held her breath. None of the cowboys worked this late. Could it be a trespasser? She'd never had to defend herself before. Her knuckles tightened around the lantern grip and turned nearly white. As she strode toward the stables, her heart hammered within her chest.

But her heartbeat slowed to a steady rhythm within seconds. Jesse was soothing one of the horses as she entered the barn. The corner of her mouth quirked up in surprise. He was whispering to Blue Star.

As she stepped closer, she heard his words drifting from down the aisle. He didn't seem to notice the lantern cautiously approaching him. "Do you think I'm taking it out on Loretta, Blue?"

The hay underneath her feet rustled as her boots landed in a pile a few stalls away from where Jesse stood. She swallowed hard at her dead giveaway. He turned sharply.

"What are you doing here?" His voice was rough. She couldn't understand why the sound sent a thrill up her spine.

"I thought maybe someone had been trespassing." She dared to step closer, watching him for a sign of apprehension. "Ranch hands don't usually come by the barn at this hour."

"You should go back in the house."

She gestured toward her horse instead, one arm holding the lantern high while the other one swung at her side. "What are you talking to Blue about? Is it about Loretta?"

He didn't respond. His shoulders stiffened as she drew near him.

"Jesse..." Emboldened by the letters, she decided to push her luck. If he really was the one writing them, she needed to give him a sign, right? "Do you want to go riding with me?"

"It's after dark."

"Never stopped us before." In fact, she'd spent plenty of nights racing with him after her father fell asleep when they were teens. "I was planning to go for a ride anyway. Do you want to accompany me?"

"Reckon I better not..."

Her stomach plummeted. She'd been so sure he was the one sending the letters. Their recent suppers together even seemed friendly. But now he'd turned cold once more. Who was she sharing her heart with?

"I just want to be friends, Jesse. Can we?"

Still no response. At least she'd tried. Evelyn nibbled her bottom lip and reached out to pet Blue Star. Jesse drew back at the gesture. She opened the stall door to let her horse trot out.

"I can ride for a little while," he conceded.

She gave a small smile as she heard him ready his own horse. His tone was wary, but she would take it. Her voice perked up. "We can check on the new barbed wire fence, too, and see how it is holding up."

Jesse made a gruff sound of approval. The two of them trotted their horses out of the stable. She brought her horse to a canter across the pasture, and he did the same.

The night air sent a chill through her, but she'd never felt more at ease. The cotton trousers and long-sleeved woolen shirt kept her warmer than any mass of skirts and shawls ever had. The comfort she felt extended beyond physical protection from the cold. She'd finally broken through to Jesse.

She glanced at him out of the corner of her eye, half expecting him to be riding away from her already. He matched her pace instead, staring straight ahead toward the fence at the edge of the ranch.

The horses whinnied as they trotted close to the barbed wire. She calmed Blue Star, stroking the wide bridge of her horse's nose. Blue sidestepped away from the wire, lifting her muscular legs a safe distance from the threatening spikes.

After Blue settled down, Evelyn shifted out of the saddle. Jesse had just stepped off his own horse and held out his hand for her to take. She nearly laughed. It had been years since a man held out his hand to help her down from a horse. She pushed it away and hit the ground herself. Her gaze turned from his hand to the new fence. The soft green grass rustled beneath her boots as she stepped toward a grueling week's work. The boys had spent all week pulling the wire tightly against the posts and hammering nails into place.

"Only problem is that the cows keep pressing against it and not realizing the damage till they've been cut up." Jesse kneeled down and pulled one end of the wire to check that the nails were in place. He ran his finger lightly against one of the tips. "I don't like them much."

"All the new ranches have them, though. We have to keep up if we plan to turn Breighton around." She knelt down next to him and mimicked his motion of testing the wire. "The cattle are going through a testing period with it. Give them time. Soon enough they will all learn to stay away. Worth the investment, I think."

She leaned over to the other side of the barbed wire to check the tautness he had been testing. She didn't realize she was checking that side at the same time he was examining the other end. They both reached forward to check the same section of wire, bumping into each other in the process. The force sent him reeling backward as her weight pinned him to the ground.

Her eyes widened. She was sure he could hear her heart beating furiously through her shirt. Her lips were only inches away from his. Even during his days as a ranch hand, before leaving for California, his lips always looked so soft. The corded muscles of his jaw clenched. Against her will, she found herself drawn closer and closer to him.

The feel of his body underneath her was so wonderfully familiar, even after all the years apart. His hard muscle beneath her soft curves made her long for increased contact. Heat pooled in the pit of her stomach. So much heat. Warmth radiated off his chest. Without thinking, she arched against him.

He slid out from underneath her. His breath came out in ragged gasps as he backed away. Evelyn fell to the ground with a hard *thud*, and a plume of dirt rose up as soon as she hit the ground.

"I'm sorry, I… Something just came over me." She dusted off her wool trousers to hide what she was sure was a sweeping blush. "I should have been more careful."

Jesse just nodded and headed in the direction of the horses. His pace was brisk, as if he couldn't get away fast enough.

She sighed as she stared at his retreating form. What had she been thinking?

She hadn't been thinking, not at all. Evelyn shut her eyes, the embarrassment washing over her in waves. This was what happened when she didn't rationalize her actions. *So much for a night ride.* All her attempts at friendship seemed to end in the same way: with him walking away from her. She wasn't sorry she'd landed on him.

She was sorry she couldn't reach out to him.

# CHAPTER FIVE

Jesse sighed. "Preston, you know I have to do what's right for my sister—"

"And that apparently involves ignoring her wishes. Got it, Greenwood." His friend let out a low huff. He stuffed his hands into his pockets and scuffed his boots against the dirt. "Don't like it, but I get it. That doctor's son gonna amount to more than I ever will. Just seems funny to me."

"What do you mean?"

"Being a ranch hand used to be enough for you." Preston spit on the ground, and Jesse had a strong feeling Preston actually wanted to spit at him. "You used to talk about running away with Evelyn and making a living being a cowboy. You never had a problem with our way of life then."

He rubbed his jaw. "That was a long time ago."

"So you've changed?"

"I grew up."

Preston remained silent. He brought his arms over the posts of the corral, staring out at the ranch. Jesse wanted to apologize, but he wasn't sure what he would be apologizing for. He remembered when he had spoken those words to Preston. That vision of the future had only existed when seen with the clarity of a sixteen-year-old.

Preston whistled long and low. "There's nothing she can't do on the ranch. Is she fixin' up that wire by herself?"

Jesse narrowed his eyes out at the pastures. Evelyn was kneeling against the wire, a hammer in one hand and the other hand pressed against the post. It was closer to the house than the barbed wire they'd inspected the other night, but that didn't make the job any easier. Surely she wasn't putting up a barbed wire by herself. He scanned the area surrounding her. To his surprise, no one else was there. Usually two men handled that wire: one stretched it while the other nailed it to the nearest post.

Together he and Preston approached Evelyn.

"We can handle it for you."

She looked up at the sound of Preston's voice. Sweat beaded down the side of her forehead, and she wiped it away with her shirt sleeve. Her eyes caught Jesse's.

Suddenly, the sun's heat seemed a whole lot hotter.

She tore her gaze away to consider Preston's offer. "Sure could use a hand. One of you needs to milk the cows. Denny usually does that, but he said he was sick today."

"I'll do it."

Before Jesse could respond, Preston had already scooted off in the direction of the barn.

She didn't look up at Jesse, though. He watched her work, her thin arms somehow whacking the hammer against the post with more masculine strength than most of the ranch hands. He picked up the wire, stretching it out so it was easier for her to nail.

"Thanks." She nodded and brushed a lock of hair behind her ear before she began hammering again. Her black hair was tucked neatly in the back, but her hat was off, leaving the loose tendrils to frame her pronounced cheekbones. She'd lost weight. Working on the land hadn't been kind to her. Still, the apples of her cheeks flushed, and she grinned when the nail was secured. For someone who'd been educated at one of those fancy East Coast seminaries, he'd never seen anyone look more fulfilled performing physical labor than Evelyn.

The sun rose high above them, and the rays beat down on the back of Evelyn's neck. She unbuttoned the top of her shirt, allowing the wind to caress more of the creamy skin at the nape of her neck. Jesse's Adam's apple bobbed up and down as he gulped at the sight. They worked in silence for a few minutes. Well, she worked. He just held up the wire against the post and tried desperately not to look at her.

When they'd finished at least half of the posts, she stepped back to admire her handiwork. She clapped her hands together, dusting them off. Jesse lifted a nearby canteen and passed it over to her. She grabbed the canteen with eagerness, gulping down the water as if she would otherwise die of thirst if she wasted a single second.

"Thank you." She handed him back the container. "You know, I always used to watch you work on the ranch and wonder what it was like."

"And what do you think?"

"I think it suits me." She let out an unladylike snort and placed her hands on her hips. "I like getting my hands dirty more than I ever thought I would. I always thought I would pursue an academic career, you know? But I've realized the right career for me is here, managing the ranch. Suits me better than reading indoors or studying piano ever did."

"I always thought so."

"You did?" Evelyn beamed with pride. Her eyes shone in the light of the sun, the specks of gold in her emerald eyes gleaming. The orbs of her eyes were nearly as green as the pastures rolling in the hills behind her. "Did you always?"

"Yes, I did." Jesse took a few sips from the canteen and placed it back on the ground next to one of the posts. When he stood, he noticed she was still staring at him with that same expectant expression of hers.

"When did you first think so?"

He shifted his weight. "Remember when I taught you how to ride? Reckoned you were a cowboy to the manner born."

She brushed a stray tendril of hair behind her ear and laughed at his question. "Of course I do. My father was so shocked to see a girl not riding sidesaddle. That was the first real time I ever talked to you, too. I miss that sometimes, you know? The innocence. The childhood that came before responsibilities."

"Before society placed you in a certain class," he added.

She considered his words for a moment. "There is one thing I never understood about childhood, though."

"What?"

"I never understood what they always told us about growing older, that everything would make more sense, that we would understand the world infinitely more. 'You will understand when you are older.' Well, I am older." She threw her hands in the air, an exasperated expression on her face. "Twenty-three and I barely understand myself, let alone anything else!"

Jesse couldn't help himself. He threw back his head and laughed for the first time in a long time. "You're right," he agreed. "There's something else I never understood either."

She smiled. "What was it?"

"How on earth folks manage to wear those pinching fancy dress shoes." He shook his head, with what he hoped was a solemn expression on his face. "Cowboy boots are all I wore here, and cowboy boots were all I ever wore in that hotel in California."

This time it was her turn to laugh. "I can just imagine you strutting about that hotel, owning the place among some high-class guests, marching around in your dust-covered black stovetop boots."

"Hey, those dust-covered boots are comfortable," he protested. A grin spread on his face. Knowing he'd made her laugh made him throw his shoulders back just a bit more. "Wore them around so much that the rest of the hotel staff started to wear 'em, too."

"No!" She giggled. For a moment, he could have sworn they were sixteen again. "I would pay anything to see that sight. What is your hotel like out there in California?"

"Sure a lot different from here, that's for sure." He sighed, folding his arms. "Wasn't easy to start out there, but as soon as the manager died and left me the place, money started to flow into my pocket pretty quickly."

"But what is it like?" Evelyn bent down again and lifted up the wire. This time he took up a nail and hammer and started securing the wire against the post. He felt her curious gaze on him, imploring him for more information.

"Looks a lot like your house, to be honest. Just a big, nice house where people would stay on their way up further north. The rich folks, I mean." He glanced down at Evelyn. "The ones who looked disapprovingly at cowboy boots."

He could have sworn she winked. "I certainly would not have looked disapprovingly at them."

"No, because you'd be wearing the outfit you have on now."

She took her free hand to pinch her shirt's calico cloth between her forefinger and thumb. "I bet I would. How would they receive me, Jesse?"

"A lady strutting around in cowboy boots, britches, and a calico shirt? They would look at you like you came from the moon. Should have taken you along with me to California. You would have given those guests a real fright."

Evelyn stood up to her full height. She looked up at him through the tops of her full lashes. A look that was far from just friendship. "Maybe you should have."

His heart lurched against his own will as he watched her walk back toward the house. *You need to stay on your guard*, he reminded himself. She'd broken his heart before; could he trust her again?

"Maybe we should also grab something to eat," she called over her shoulder.

And maybe there was hope for a second chance.

# CHAPTER SIX

Evelyn entertained images of Jesse Greenwood's strong arms around her narrow waist as she walked to the barn. The cows in their stalls didn't seem to care what romantic ideas were running through her head. She picked up the cool metal pail from the corner of the barn and hauled it to the first of the stalls.

At the end of the aisle, she caught a glimpse of a man smoking a cigarette and leaning against the closed stall door. She scowled as soon as she recognized him.

"Denny!" She marched over to the ranch hand. By the time she reached him, the incriminating cigarette was out of his hands, probably discarded somewhere in the haystacks. "You're not milking the cows today. Where should you be?"

"Helping set up the fence posts, ma'am." Denny slumped his shoulders.

"I do not ever want to see you neglecting your work again, you hear me?"

He mumbled something under his breath, averting his eyes from hers.

She raised her voice. "I said, did you hear me?"

"I heard you, ma'am."

"Go help set up those fence posts right now!"

"Yes, ma'am." Denny slunk away, down the aisle and toward the barn door.

"If I catch you hiding away from your chores again I will not hesitate to let you go next time!" she called out. As soon as the barn door swung shut behind him, she shook her head. Breighton had barely begun to turn a profit. She couldn't risk paying the wages of inefficient ranch hands.

Evelyn returned to the business of milking cows. She heard a small sound coming from where Denny had stood, but she ignored it. *Probably one of the cows just being restless.*

The cow shifted in place as she approached her. "Calm down," she soothed. "It's only me." Her hands gripped the udders and squeezed downward into the metal bucket below.

Her thoughts wandered to the mysterious man behind the letters. The notes had increased in frequency as the friendship between them grew. They even shared multiple letters a day sometimes. Other suitors had expressed interest in her in the past, of course, especially the ever-patient John, but these letters were filled with such longing and intimacy. Jesse was the only possible man she knew that could have written them.

But he wasn't the kind of man to deny the truth when caught. Or at least he wasn't before he left for California. Who knew, now? Evelyn sniffed the air. *Strange.* A scent she couldn't quite place filled her nostrils. It was a mix of old hay and something else entirely. An odd smell filled the barn. It wasn't manure either; it was something richer.

She continued to milk the cow until the pail filled to the brim. *There.* Another chore crossed off the list. She picked up the large pail and stood to begin the trek back to the house. Yet that charred scent still lingered in the air. She scanned the area, searching for the source of the smell. There was nothing odd in the stall.

She pushed open the stall door, trying not to swing the pail in her hands. The smell persisted. It increased with each passing moment, the pungent scent reminding her of a fireplace.

The hairs on the back of her neck bristled. The aisle was completely normal, but the animals in the barn grew restless. Horses bucked wildly in their stalls. More sounds accompanied the animals' vocal fear. A crackling noise struck behind her, and sudden whooshes of air accompanied the sound of a blaze building. Evelyn gulped.

*Smoke.* The smell was smoke.

The metal pail clanged to the floor, white milk spilling across the hay in all directions. Her hands lay slack at her sides, ignoring the bucket rolling on the ground in front of her.

"Fire!" she screamed.

• • •

Jesse matched Mr. Lancaster's slow stride across the cleared dirt road. "I cannot thank you enough for working as a ranch hand at Breighton for free. Of course I'll get you your cut of the profit, but I do appreciate your help," the old man said grudgingly. Jesse could tell every word cost his new business partner another piece of his soul.

Jesse waved his hand and stepped forward. The chill of the air made him fold his hands across his chest to conserve heat. "I grew up on this ranch, Mr. Lancaster. Can't see it fall apart."

"Even so." Mr. Lancaster stopped walking as soon as they reached the fences. He rested his hand against the post for support before they continued back toward the house. "You'll see your first profit payment when…" Suddenly, his lips parted, and his widened eyes flickered from Jesse to something behind him.

Jesse leaned forward, waiting for the rest of the sentence. "Everything all right, Mr. Lancaster?"

"Good Lord!" His eyes filled with terror. "The barn!"

Jesse whipped his head around.

One side of the barn was ablaze, while ranch hands gathered outside to try to contain the fire. A line had formed from the well, and desperate pails of water were passed along to put out the rising blaze. Most fearsome was the thick smoke drifting from the entrance of the barn. It permeated everywhere, causing the cowboys closest to the blaze to lift their shirts over their mouths to guard against the fiery air.

Someone had raced inside long enough to let the animals out of their stalls, because nearly all the cows were clustered outside the barn. Several of the horses bucked wildly as smoke filled the air, whinnying as cowboys barely hung onto the reins of the animals to keep them from escaping. Other cowboys rounded up the frightened cattle that had been scared enough to break out of the herd.

Jesse raced forward.

Denny, the youngest ranch hand, was at the center of a group of cowboys. Someone was trying to calm him down, but he just kept shaking his head no matter what the boys said to him.

He flinched as Jesse grabbed his shirt lapels, yanking him into the air.

"What happened? What started the fire?"

"It was… it was my fault." Denny sniffed and shuddered. His eyes were wide in fear. "I was so mad that Miss had caught me smoking, I thought I'd just leave my cigarette in the hay and let her stamp it out for me…"

Jesse's stomach plummeted. "Miss? Miss who?"

He stopped sniffling to look up in confusion. "Why, Miss Lancaster, of course." He gasped.

"God, she's still in there! Miss Lancaster's still in that barn!"

Dread filled the pit of his gut as his worst fear was confirmed. Jesse spun around to take in the sight of the burning building. The blaze was probably worse inside. A whooshing sound echoed through his ears as flames fanned into the evening air.

He scanned the crowd around him and cursed beneath his breath. No sign of Evelyn anywhere. There was no way she would be cooped up in the house when her barn was burning. The animals had been moved to safety, but she had been left inside.

Without ceremony, Jesse dropped Denny. The ranch hand fell to the ground with a whimper. Jesse felt nothing but disgust toward him. He ran from Denny to the front of the water bucket brigade. The ranch hands seemed to be making at least slow progress toward putting out the blaze, but it wouldn't be enough to save anyone inside. Anything inside would be burned to a crisp.

Jesse gritted his teeth. *Or anyone.*

His body snapped back as another pair of hands grabbed him. He attempted to shrug off the hands, but the person holding onto him had a firm grip. His attacker turned Jesse around and placed both hands onto his shoulders.

A familiar voice growled at him. "Where do you think you're going?"

"I have to get inside the barn!"

"Oh no, you ain't. You can't go in there!" Fieldings, the oldest ranch hand, scowled at Jesse. "Not if you want to live, Greenwood. Help the men from outside."

He pushed Fieldings off, who staggered back. "Evelyn Lancaster is still in that barn!"

Fieldings grabbed Jesse by the neck of his shirt and glared. "Trying to get yourself killed?" he asked. "Look here, I want Miss Lancaster saved as much as anyone. But we don't want to lose two lives today instead of one. Ain't no glory in that, Greenwood. Save yourself and the barn and the animals first, then we'll get Miss Lancaster."

Jesse recoiled and shoved the man's hands off his shirt. He wouldn't be able to live with himself if he let her die. He raced toward the entrance of the barn as his mind registered the protests of the men from outside. Jesse pushed open the barn door and jumped inside. As soon as he entered, he pulled up his wool shirt to cover his mouth and nose against the fumes. The large barn door swung shut behind him, as if trapping him to confirm the consequences of his perilous choice. No time to think twice. Pure instinct drove his body forward further toward the flames.

Smoke filled every crevice of the building. The gray cloud permeated the outside air as well, but with the concentration of the wooden slats surrounding all sides of the barn, the effect was even more disorienting and daunting inside. He could barely see the stalls around him and rafters above him. The cloud of smoke was too dense to make out anything except blurred outlines and vivid flames.

While the fire seemed contained to only one side from the front, inside the barn was a different story. Smoke began to filter through his fabric. He coughed as he inspected the damage. Orange and yellow waves danced across his line of vision. Crackling flames licked every corner. Colors merged to create an even more confusing path in front of him.

Some of the stalls had already burned down, and he could no longer make out the aisle inside the barn. There was only fire and dry ground. The only constant was the cloud of grey vapor covering every visible nook and cranny.

"Evelyn!" he yelled, and then covered his mouth and nose again.

No response.

His coughing doubled as the persistent smoke still found a way through the material to settle in his lungs. He looked up. Several of the beams holding the barn together had caught ablaze. The rafters were not just on fire; they were drooping, the blaze eroding away the shaky beams that held them.

He ran forward before a beam could cut off his path and start another blaze. Another beam fell where he had previously stood right as he jumped out of the way. He swore under his breath. The burning beam narrowly missed the entrance, if he was making out the shape of the wood against the smoke correctly. It would be a matter of only minutes until the blaze blocked the entryway as well.

He leaped over the patches of blazing hay to avoid the remaining stalls covered in flames. Really, the whole place was nothing more than a roaring fireplace. His heart sank. If Evelyn had been unconscious in one of those stalls, there was no way she could survive.

"Eve!" he roared. He barely heard his own voice over the sound of the flames, much less any other noise.

The farther he went inside the barn, the harder it would be to get out. Still, there was no sign of her. He walked forward again, narrowing his eyes to focus against the smoke for any shape of life.

He heard coughing again, but this time Jesse knew it wasn't his. The coughing grew louder, and he stepped toward the source of the sound.

A figure stumbled forward around a corner and into his path, supporting its weight on only one foot. A figure with long, dark hair.

"Evelyn!"

She looked up. Her brow furrowed. While she opened her mouth to respond, coughing came out instead. She clutched her hand over her mouth. Then she tripped over the end of a beam and fell forward, her knees slamming against the ground.

Pushing through the cloud of smoke, Jesse darted forward, dodging another falling beam as he hurried toward the figure.

Her body lay crumpled on the floor, completely unconscious and thus unaware of the blaze at the end of the beam coming closer to her. He lifted her up just as the end of the beam transformed to flames, morphing the previously harmless wood into a deadly obstacle.

Her eyes fluttered open for only a second. He could barely make out her wheezing gasps through the sounds of the blaze.

Her red cotton dress was torn from her fall, the hem now dragging on the ground. He ripped away the fire hazard and chucked the unnecessary fabric to the ground before picking Evelyn up, bridal style, and carrying her toward the rapidly deteriorating entrance.

With his hands occupied, Jesse tried his best not to breathe the deadly air around him. But he couldn't stop the desperate coughing from starting again as smoke burned the length of his throat. He felt like someone was setting him on fire from within his own body as he struggled to remain upright and grounded on a path to the door.

The first beam that fell nearly covered the entire entrance of the barn, but he could see some of the flames at the end of the wall were reduced. The fire had removed the entrance door. Checking to see if his next step was straight into a burning wooden post, he narrowed his eyes against the vapor clouding his vision and stepped over the end of a beam. The path was clear. Swinging her in his arms, he ran.

Bright light filled his vision, and his lungs gasped in the fresh air to flush out the smoke. Flames no longer danced in front of his eyes. He'd never been happier to see so much dry dirt in front of him.

He set Evelyn's limp body down until her feet touched the ground. Her head bobbed to the side, her eyes shut and face covered in soot. Her dress was even more damaged than he'd realized in the barn, and he couldn't tell if the dress merely looked darker in some areas or if the stains were blood.

"I think she's hurt," he rasped to the maid who met him. Even with the outside air rushing into his lungs, his throat felt covered in ash. "Be careful."

The maid, Irene, nodded. She carried her in the direction of the big house. His heart lurched as he watched her limp body being hurried toward the house and away from him. He wanted to carry her to her room; he needed to see if she would wake up.

He started after the maid, but Fieldings grabbed him again. His familiar bark made Jesse clench his fists. "You can see her later! We need to stop this blaze!"

Jesse scowled but turned away from Evelyn and back to helping the ranch hands. He joined the line in digging dirt trenches to fight the fire from spreading. Slowly but surely, the blaze began to die. The red and orange glow licked at the corners of the end of the barn. The ranch hands stood back and let the barn collapse.

Afterward, the cowboys stood in silence in front of the smoldering ashes. Their victory at saving the livestock felt hollow—they were staring at months of work to rebuild. Mr. Lancaster gave commands to build a temporary corral for the dairy cows in the morning.

He ordered Jesse and some of the other cowboys to fetch several of the horses that had managed to bolt from the barn. Jesse found two of the mustangs and trotted them back to the temporary coral where they would stay for the night. The entire time, his mind was occupied with Evelyn's condition. Was she still unconscious?

He kept his eyes fixed on the house through most of his chores. There was a lantern light in her window—surely that was a good sign. As soon as the men finished erecting a basic skeleton of the corral, Fieldings allowed all the ranch hands to retire for the night. While the other men sneaked away to the cookhouse for a second supper, Jesse headed back to the big house.

The porch door creaked open as he stepped inside. He heard hushed voices from down the hall, where her room was. His heart thudded inside his chest, afraid of what the voices were saying about her fate. The image of her unconscious body, covered in ash, filled his mind. He stopped at her doorway, taking in the sight before him.

A doctor dabbed Evelyn's forehead with a wet cloth. Her eyes were shut, her pale cheeks matching the same shade of the white pillowcase behind her head. All the soot and dirt had been wiped off, but he couldn't see her chest rise and fall from breathing. Mr. Lancaster was standing over his daughter and the doctor, shaking his head.

"No!" Jesse yelled, rushing to her bed and kneeling down. The room started to spin. Surely she couldn't be—

He buried the thought, afraid to even put words to the dread.

"What's happening, doc?"

Mr. Lancaster answered instead. "It could've been so much worse."

"What do you mean?" His insides clenched.

His former boss's voice was low and reassuring. "Some burns here and there, and a sprained ankle. But otherwise she's going to be all right."

Jesse felt his shoulders slouch, the tenseness of his muscles slowly evaporating.

The doctor nodded in agreement. He set the washcloth down into a basin filled with water on the nightstand. "The burns won't fade, but there's no internal or physical damage that can't be fixed with some bed rest." The white-haired man wagged his finger at Mr. Lancaster. "No strenuous activity for several weeks until the ankle heals. Preventive measures. Then she'll be just fine."

Relief swelled inside his chest. He wanted to embrace the doctor. Heck, he would kiss the man, the wonderful man who told him that she was going to be just fine.

He leaned closer to her. Upon closer inspection, her expression looked peaceful. Her thick and full lashes lay pressed upon her skin, contrasting with the cool pallor of her cheeks. Her mouth spread out in a serene line, as if in the middle of a wonderful dream. He felt like someone had just lifted a boulder off his chest.

She was going to be all right.

"You saved her life, Jesse." Mr. Lancaster's voice sounded far away, so far removed from the vision of her sleeping before him. "I cannot thank you enough."

He didn't need thanks. He had all the gratitude he needed: Evelyn sleeping soundly in bed, safe and secure against the flames that had threatened to take her away from the world—from him.

He let out the breath he hadn't realized he'd been holding.

• • •

The sound of a rooster crowing caused Evelyn's eyelids to flutter open. As sunlight streamed through the window, the darkness of dreams melted away, and the sudden bright, blinding light filtering through her lids made her wince. The last thing she remembered was the barn being full of smoke and tripping over a fallen beam—and then Jesse had saved her. Or, at least, she thought so. She'd barely been able to see anything through that smoke.

A shadow fell across her face, the shape of a man near her bed. There was a terrible pain from somewhere on her leg, but the pain was momentarily forgotten as her heart soared at the thought of who stood next to her.

"Is that you?" Evelyn smiled at the profile. Jesse had come to see her. He'd saved her from the fire! Surely that was a sign that he cared for her. He was here to see her rest and get better; he was here to confess to the letters and his feelings for her.

"Yes, it is."

Her heart ran cold. The voice wasn't Jesse's at all. As her eyes adjusted to the light and she discovered who the figure was, her heart sank.

"John Cooper." Her tone was flat. "What are you doing here?"

His handsome features lit up when she said his name. John lifted off his hat and smiled down at Evelyn. She hated to admit it was a genuine smile, albeit a proud one. Unlike her other suitors, he actually cared about her, rather than simply her ranch.

"I rode here as soon as I heard you were hurt. I'm glad to see you recovering."

She sighed. It was hard to dislike a suitor who was so earnest. "Thank you, but as you can see, I am perfectly well..." She tried to swing her legs over the side of her bed, but a sharp, searing pain caused her to gasp and remain still.

John knelt down. With a soft push, he leaned her back against the pillows. "Mr. Lancaster told me you twisted your ankle. He says you need rest."

No use in attempting to escape, then. She pulled the upper half of her body against the headboard until she was sitting upright. Where was Jesse?

"Do you know the extent of the damage to the ranch?" She grimaced. She only hoped the fire was contained to the barn. Another set of added expenses, another wave of more ranch hands needed.

"It collapsed. Your father said there was nothing to be done."

She drew a quick intake of breath. *Nothing to be done.* "My father is resting, right?"

"No, actually…" John gave her a sideways glance. It was odd to see such a proud man look bashful, and his next words were spoken in a hesitating way. "Your father and the other ranch hands are needed to do the chores while some of the others repair the barn. I volunteered to take care of you."

*Just wonderful.* She suppressed the groan rising in her chest. "I assure you, I will be fine. I can take care of myself."

"Your swollen ankle doesn't seem to say so." John pointed to her leg. He dragged forward an oak chair resting against the wall closest to her, the chair legs scraping against the oak floor. He sat down, and she literally couldn't bring herself to scoot away.

"I thought you might like some company."

"I think all I need to pass the time is a nice book, really. Could you please fetch me one of my books from the library across the hall?"

After he had left the room, she glared at her treacherous ankle.

John stayed the rest of the afternoon, reading his own novel alongside Evelyn. He'd pause in his reading occasionally to ask a question about her book. Thankfully, as soon as the sun began to set, he wished her good evening and finally left. She found him surprisingly honest, even if he was vain. He seemed genuine in a way that her previous suitors hadn't.

Still, there was only so much of him she could take. When the door closed behind him, she let out a sigh of relief. His persistence almost proved too much. She brightened up considerably, however, when her father visited later. She prodded him with endless questions about the state of the ranch until he gave her detailed answers to all of them.

The sun was long down by the time her father left the room, opening the door wide enough for Evelyn to see Jesse standing next to the door. He stepped backward when her eyes met his, as if he'd been caught in the act of something terrible.

Her father nodded abruptly at him, and then inclined his head toward her. "I'm all done here. You can go in."

Jesse took off his hat as he entered the room. He looked back at the door as her father closed it, waiting for him to leave. He spoke when the door finally closed halfway.

"I was so worried about you, Eve."

The sound of her nickname soothed her more than laudanum ever could. "Father told me about how you saved me from the fire." She pursed her lips. "Not that I approve of ignoring the state of the barn."

Jesse rolled his eyes, but his solemn features cracked into a smile. His fingers traced the brim of his hat as he spoke. "Next time I'll be sure to leave you in the barn."

"Do that and I will come back from the grave and fire you on the spot, Jesse Greenwood."

"Sure would be an experience." The hard planes of his face contrasted against the curved ease of his grin. "How's life in bed?"

She lifted up the two tomes on her covers, each one weighing nearly five pounds. "Years of formal education finally came to use.

I can now bore myself all day with the collection in my father's library."

"Sounds exciting."

"A real rodeo, definitely." She patted her bed. "Sit."

He started, as if he'd considered it for a second, but then his shoulders squared again, and he stood up straighter. "That's fine. I can stand. That bed's yours. You rest on it."

Evelyn nibbled her lower lip. "I am not going to break. You can sit down on the bed. I can handle that."

He finally obeyed, but he still looked uncomfortable. He perched so gingerly on the quilt that her bed hardly shifted with his added weight. It was as if he'd entered some sacred Native American religious grounds and was under surveillance by the federal marshal at the same time. She wanted to laugh at the sight of her cowboy, who could walk into a burning barn without a second thought, yet seemed so wary of sitting on a girl's bed.

"I still cannot believe you followed me into that burning barn." She reached for his right hand and clasped it in both of hers. "Thank you."

"I would follow you anywhere if you were in trouble." His eyes flickered down at his hand. He didn't move either, just sat there with a spine ramrod straight.

"What about a corral full of stampeding bulls?"

His lips quirked upward in a smile. "Even there."

"Most people would not risk their life like that." She squeezed his hand, but his remained motionless. She was desperate for a physical sign of his affection. If not for his replies, she wouldn't have believed he cared about her at all.

"I'm not most people."

Evelyn looked up into his round brown eyes. They'd always looked so warm to her; they were what first convinced her to get to know him better. His soft, kind eyes always expressed that he was more than some rough cowboy who helped out on her father's ranch. He was different than the rest.

"You are not like anyone else," she whispered. She let go of his hand to place her own in her lap, lacing her fingers together.

His gaze followed, as if he considered grabbing them. Instead, he stood up from her bed. She couldn't help feeling a twinge of disappointment. Whoever wrote to her was so expressive in the letters. Maybe she was hoping for too much from the silent cowboy. He moved toward the glass window, his hands clasped behind his back. Strength rippled from his forearms and his defined upper biceps through the thin material of his shirt, and she longed to run her hands across his body.

She squeezed her hands in her lap instead. He probably thought she was a fool for appearing too eager.

• • •

Jesse felt like an idiot. When she'd let go of his hand, of course, he should have reached out. She'd practically given him permission when she grabbed his hand first.

But what if she hadn't? What if she were just being friendly by that gesture? Isn't that what she'd asked him a month ago—*Can't we be friends?*

He wished someone taught him how to handle women the way he was taught to handle cattle. He and Evelyn started out as friends years ago, but that was before she'd rejected him. He wanted nothing more than for someone to instruct him on the right way to talk to a woman. Or convince a woman to give him a second chance.

When he turned back around, she was staring down into her lap. Her hunched shoulders pushed her breasts against the top of her dress again. The soft flesh of her neck was exposed as well, and her dress had been pulled up above her ankles so she could inspect the swelling. He glanced down at her legs, the shapely arch of her calf tempting him without as much as a movement.

He cleared his throat. He couldn't think about satisfying the head beneath his waist if she was offering him friendship. "What books are you reading?"

She picked up one of the volumes and thumbed through the yellowed pages. "Both are absolutely boring and make me wonder how soon my ankle will heal. I'm just lonely during the day, mostly. I miss the outdoors." She set the book down, and then hope sparkled in her eyes. "You will visit me tomorrow, will you not?"

"I've got work to do on the ranch all day…" His voice trailed off at the droop in her shoulders. "But I'm sure I can make some time."

"No, I cannot believe I even asked." She gestured to the window, or what Jesse assumed was really the remains of the barn outside. "If I were up and able, I would spend all my time fixing that barn. With our ranch hands low, Father and the other boys need all the help they can get. I will be fine here on my own." A small smile broke out at the corner of her mouth. "Let us see how many more books will put me to sleep before my ankle heals."

He chuckled, but his heart ached at the thought of her here alone. He could probably make some time to see her during the day, he reckoned.

True to his plan, he hurried through his chores the next day. Fieldings was preoccupied with lifting a beam back into the rafters long enough for Jesse to slip away from the other cowboys and back toward the big house.

He even picked some honeysuckle from one of the pastures near the ranch. If she couldn't go outside, he'd bring the outdoors to her.

His footsteps slowed when he heard the sound of a familiar masculine voice inside her bedroom. *John Cooper.* His brow furrowed. What was the judge's son doing here? He paused near the doorway, trying to hear the conversation inside.

The voices were too faint for him to make out, though. He peered in the room instead, his body safely hidden behind the door.

John Cooper laughed at something Evelyn had said, responding in an animated way, with wide hand gestures and exaggerated expressions across his delighted face.

Whatever he'd said, it made Evelyn laugh, too. Her forgotten books laid haphazardly to the side of her bedspread, probably chucked in a hurry when John had entered the room.

Jesse glared at the scene. His only knowledge of the man was seeing him with the judge and hearing Loretta's raving about how handsome he was. John Cooper was clean-shaven and polished. White shirt, black coat, fancy dress shoes. Upper class. Good family. East Coast education. Everything Jesse wasn't.

He clenched his fists as he watched the two talk. John responded to Evelyn immediately, with smooth ease. His shoulders were relaxed, and he even patted her hand a few times during their conversation.

Jesse didn't need to torture himself anymore. John Cooper knew how to talk to a woman, and the woman he'd chosen was Evelyn. His intentions were as clear as day.

He swallowed hard. Evelyn was no fool. Surely she could tell John was sweet on her. But what did she see in him? His body was too weak to help her out on the ranch. Everyone knew he couldn't shoot a door in a duel, though he bragged about his pistol. He wasn't even that handsome.

Jesse walked back down the hallway, but paused before a small basin filled with water. He gazed down at his reflection. He'd never spent much time worrying about his appearance. The scruff on his chin had gone unmanaged for a while and he'd let his beard grow out longer than he had before. A smear of dirt had somehow gone unnoticed across the bridge of his nose. He swiped it away, but it didn't change his appearance. Even with his newfound wealth in California, it didn't change who he really was: a cowboy.

John Cooper, meanwhile, was a well-bred judge's son. He could spend all day talking about academics with Evelyn, or reminisce about their time near the Atlantic. They were of the same class; they had blue-blooded upbringings in common.

All she wanted from Jesse was friendship. None of the letters he'd received from her were addressed to anyone in particular. She still had no idea it was him.

The honeysuckle crushed in his hand as he clenched his fist. She clearly didn't even care about the letters. Jesse stormed out of the house and back to the ranch chores with new purpose. At the back of his mind, he knew his efforts were useless.

No amount of cattle herding or fence mending was going to get his Eve out of his mind.

# CHAPTER SEVEN

"Father, have you seen Jesse?" Evelyn laid her fork down next to her plate. She hadn't seen him all day. She hadn't seen him in the last few days, actually. "Does he not eat in the house anymore?"

"You've been in bed for the last two weeks, Evelyn. He's been eating in the cookhouse with the other cowboys lately. Works himself way too hard for this ranch."

She frowned. "Why does he eat in the cookhouse now?"

"Blend in with the boys. He's more than fulfilled his end of the bargain by investing in the ranch, but he's serious about not letting any of the other ranch hands know about his part in saving Breighton. Says he wants to be just another cowboy back on the ranch again while he's here."

She pursed her lips. That was probably why he hadn't visited her in the last week, she reasoned with herself. He was busy with work on the ranch. She smothered worries of his waning interest. "Do we still keep his room at the big house?"

"Oh, sure. He still sleeps here. He just prefers to take his meals somewhere else." Her father shrugged. "Whatever suits him is fine with me."

Evelyn patted the edge of her mouth with her napkin and then placed it beside her plate. She scooted her chair out from the table and excused herself. After a nod from her father, she headed toward the porch. She opened the front door and stepped onto the porch. No ranch work for at least another two weeks, the doctor ordered, but Evelyn was just grateful to be able to go outside again.

She breathed in the fresh air like it was the first time she'd ever done so. The dry Texan heat of dusk comforted her. Being inside for too long made her feel trapped, and deprived. She had only her father and John to keep her company. She'd written to Jesse as soon as she'd been able to get out of bed, and placed the letter in the tree knothole, her heart hammering in her chest thinking of his possible reply.

Tonight her letter was gone. Someone had taken it away and read it.

Yet there was no reply.

She frowned. There was always a reply.

The back-and-forth motion of the oak rocker she rested against gave her some semblance of peace on the porch. She placed her elbow on one of the wooden chair arms and rested her cheek in her palm. Her head tilted slightly, eyes fixed the tree knothole where her letter had been laid. Maybe one of the other ranch hands had picked it up. Her heart hammered in her chest. Who else could have the letter?

A pair of familiar, newfangled leather chaps and iron spurs entered her line of vision. Her gaze followed up the line of high-stitched scalloped cowboy boots and into Jesse's gaze. She smiled.

"Hello, Jesse."

He didn't smile in return.

"Hello, Evelyn."

Her gut tightened when she heard the formal address of her name once more. Why did he seem so solemn all of a sudden?

"What happened to 'Eve', hmm?"

Her hand brushed past his. He recoiled at the touch, as if her hand would burn him. She suppressed the urge to sigh. Lately she'd been nothing but walking on eggshells around him. Was she being too forward again?

"Seems like your ankle healed."

Evelyn looked down at the bandage, and then turned a sharp look back up to him. Did he really not want to see her while she was recovering? She curled the hand he'd scorned around the end of one of the chair arms. Even John had visited her, several times. She bit her lip.

"Why did you not visit me the past two weeks?"

His shoulders straightened. He stared directly ahead instead of at her. When he finally spoke, his tone sounded indifferent. "I had work to do."

Her lips parted. She could see the tensed muscles corded up in Jesse's forearm. His fists weren't clenched, but he was hardly at ease. "You could have visited, at least once. I have not seen you at all—"

"Surely you understand all the work required on the ranch."

"I wanted you to visit. I was worried something happened to you." Her brow furrowed. "Are you ignoring me?"

He swallowed, but looked at her. His brown eyes, which had once gazed so warmly in her direction, seemed cold as ice now. "I don't know what you're talking about."

"I feel like we are just running in circles. I offer my friendship to you, and you shut me out." She swallowed to prevent herself from mentioning the letters. It seemed impossible that all the tender words of love expressed so eloquently could come from the same man whose tone was now as icy as an East Coast blizzard. Clearly he possessed no feelings of emotional attachment toward her. "I know we cannot help but think about what happened between us in the past, but we can put that behind us."

She could see the hairs bristle on the back of his neck. He nodded curtly. "I've never let the past get in the way of working the ranch."

*Lies*, Evelyn wanted to reply. His perfect indifference infuriated her. "Are you playing games with me? You are nice to me one minute, and then you ignore me the next."

She saw him flex his right hand, as if exercising self-restraint. He opened his mouth, but nothing came out.

*Say something!* She wanted to yell it so loudly that all the neighboring ranches of Texas would hear her and telegram to tell her to be quiet. She wanted to exclaim the words until Jesse finally communicated with her.

"Good night," he muttered. His boots clipped against the wooden floorboards as he swung open the porch door and stepped inside the house.

•••

Evelyn wasn't able to sleep that night. She tossed and turned, burying her hands beneath her pillow. Her mind filled with possible solutions for his silence. He wouldn't express his feelings to her in person, but there had to be a way to reach out to him.

The only communication she seemed to have with him anymore was through the letters. *Better than nothing.*

Hours after midnight, she took out a pen and paper to confess her confusion and detail her disappointment. She stuffed the letter into an envelope and placed it in the knothole. Hopefully he'd see it in the morning before he went to work on the ranch. The sooner he saw the letter, the sooner they'd be back to normal.

It was midday when Evelyn dared to venture out to the tree knothole again. If Jesse really had received her letter, it would be gone by now. She put on her best dress and tied her hair up neatly. Her mouth pursed at her reflection and her hands smoothed over the front ruffles of her green dress with white piping. Maybe he would be waiting on her porch again, ready to finally admit his feelings toward her.

But what if she'd made up all of their moments in her head? She twirled a lock of hair around her finger as she stepped off the porch and into her front yard. Maybe Jesse didn't write those letters after all—

Her train of thought was interrupted by the sight before her.

Standing there, holding an envelope with a broken seal in one hand and reading her long letter from the other, was John Cooper.

He scanned her words of love like a bear drooling over a stash of honey without a hive guarding it. His blue eyes were as wide as saucers. Disbelief, joy, and appreciation passed over his expression in alternating cycles.

"John Cooper?" At her interruption, his gaze darted from her to the letter in his hand. She gulped. There had to be a logical explanation. She stepped forward with caution, as if coming too close would only confirm her nightmare. "Why are you holding that letter?"

"Who did you write this letter for?" John smiled at her, his features lighting up. He shook the paper as if he'd found some great prize. "You write here that you give the addressee full permission to court you—to whom is this addressed to?"

"The man who leaves me letters." Evelyn felt her palms gather perspiration. The way John held the letter frightened her, as if he owned the envelope and the letter and her. "I found the first note addressed to me, and I have kept a correspondence with the person who writes them."

John glanced back at the letter. He seemed to be considering something, his forehead creased with concentration as he read over her words again. Her cheeks burned. She wanted nothing more than to snatch the letter right out of his grasp. Those words weren't meant for him!

Finally, he folded the letter and placed it in his pocket. There was an odd look of determination in his eyes, as if he'd mulled something over and finally made up his mind. "Do you like them? These letters sent to you?"

Her eyes rested on the pocket of his vest. "I do."

He ran his thumb across the bottom of his jaw and sighed. "I must admit, I did not expect you to find my secret so directly. Evelyn, I am the man who writes you these letters."

Her jaw dropped. Surely there was a mistake. Those letters were from Jesse, weren't they? "If those letters are from you, where was the first letter placed? It wasn't in the knothole."

"Of course not. I placed it…" He hesitated for a moment, and then his eyes lit up. "I placed it on the porch."

Her heart sank. She'd been deluding herself the entire time.

As if he'd known that he'd entered her thoughts, Jesse suddenly passed by the tree. He gripped the worn saddle horn as his black mustang trotted past the house. Surely he could see her, even out of the corner of his eye. She stood as plain as day in front of him! But he ignored her just the same.

Her gaze flipped from the cowboy who couldn't seem to care less about her to the earnest man standing before her. Now John was holding her hand, his well-manicured fingers gripping hers for dear life. "I was the one who wrote you the love letters. I've wanted to court you for so long. Tell me my hope has not been in vain, Evelyn Lancaster."

She found she didn't even have the heart to remove her hand from John's grasp. Her eyes trailed after Jesse's retreating form. The corners of her eyes stung with saltwater tears. Foolish hopes; that was all she'd pinned on him. Once again, she'd let her imagination get the better of her. She'd even imagined he had feelings for her.

She blinked back the tears threatening to fall and wished for an escape hole to suddenly appear beneath her black buckled boots. "I… I do not know what to say."

"Promise me you'll let me court you, in the proper fashion and approved by your father." John Cooper gripped her other hand, and she felt the uncomfortable sensation of his hands squeezing both of hers. She doubted she could run away even if she tried. "I will make you the happiest woman in Hamilton."

She wanted to laugh. Promises. What good had a promise ever done her?

*Turn around,* she wanted to call to Jesse. She squinted at his profile heading down the trail. If he turned around in three seconds, then he did care for her. She hadn't been imagining his feelings for her. Desperate hopes bubbled in her heart.

*Three…*

*Two…*

"Turn around," she whispered beneath her breath.

*One.*

Evelyn bit her lower lip so hard she tasted blood. "I accept your proposal."

"What did you say?" John asked.

With a lifeless voice, she repeated, "Yes. You may court me."

John dropped her hands in surprise and grinned. "You will not regret this, Miss Evelyn Lancaster. You are worth the wait. Our future marriage will be the most lavish affair Texas has ever seen. I want you to be happy."

She wanted to be sick.

She spun around, retreating back into the safety of her home. She didn't know what had possessed her in that moment. It didn't matter anymore who she was with.

Every man was now the same to her.

Even Jesse Greenwood.

•••

Jesse turned his head back in the direction of the tree. Evelyn was no longer standing there. John remained instead, the tall man pacing up and down the porch with excitement. His hands were clasped behind his back, the black leather gloves making him look even more ridiculous than normal.

Why had Evelyn been speaking so intently with John, anyway? Jesse thought back to earlier that afternoon. He'd ridden toward the porch when he saw Evelyn emerge from the house. But John beat him to her in the yard, and Evelyn didn't seem to mind. She even looked *glad* to see John.

Jesse had ridden away as soon as he saw them together. Clearly Evelyn hadn't wanted to be disturbed. She'd seen him riding past the tree and said nothing, just ignored him as if she couldn't be bothered to speak with him when she was with John.

He scowled, turning his head back around to urge the horse into a gallop. Why had he even looked? Clearly all she needed was John Cooper to keep her company.

"Giddyap!" He removed his hat to slap the wide brim across the horse's rump. The horse followed his command as he weaved down the road and toward Loretta's house.

The house he'd purchased for Loretta stood on the outskirts of Hamilton, but not as far as Breighton and not nearly as isolated. The trail only continued for another ten minutes until it reached Hamilton's main avenue. The house was large enough to fit four people comfortably, and without the added acres around the property to manage, the upkeep wasn't much at all. The blue house had white shingles, a small porch, and—Jesse furrowed his brow. Two maids running around the front?

He slowed his horse to a halt and stepped out of the stirrups. He'd barely set his feet on the ground before one of the maids rushed toward him.

He stepped back as she flung her arms around him, instantly wetting his shirt as she cried into his chest. She howled, shaking her head against his shirt as if he were already wrong before he'd even supplied a word. He slowly pulled her back from his soaked cotton shirt and placed both of his hands on her shoulders. "What's wrong?"

"It's Loretta!" The maid wailed again and wiped her tears with the side of one of her sleeves. "She's run away."

His heart stopped cold. "What?"

"She's gone!" The woman threw out her arms into the air, a defeated expression on her face. "One moment I was clipping her clothes on the hanger to dry, the next moment I come in her room to check on her and she's fled the house!"

"How do you know?"

"She left this note." The maid pulled out a piece of scrap paper. He grabbed the note from her and instantly recognized Loretta's handwriting. The curly, looping letters seemed to taunt him with the carefree way she wrote. His face blanched as he read.

Jesse,

I have decided to take my future into my own hands. Preston and I are going to elope. Do not even try to send the sheriff after me, for I will have left Hamilton before you even read this note. Preston and I are going where you cannot stop us. I do not wish to remain trapped in a loveless marriage or always regret giving up on my love, no matter how financially comfortable I will be. I will not repeat your mistake. Give the doctor's son my best regards.

He rubbed his jaw. He didn't imagine her behavior would ever come to this. He crushed the letter in his hand. The foolish girl. If anyone in town found out about this, she'd be ruined.

After thanking the maid, he stuffed the crumpled paper into his pocket and galloped back to Breighton. When the horse finally pulled up to a stop in front of the ranch, the clearing was empty. He couldn't help but feel a small wave of relief that John Cooper's horse was gone.

Jesse leaped off his mustang and stormed straight to the door of the big house. There was no time to lose. The longer he waited, the farther away Loretta could be. He needed to speak to Mr. Lancaster about this.

The door was locked. He wrapped his knuckles hard against the wooden door. "Mr. Lancaster! I need to speak to you immediately."

When the door swung open, Evelyn stood there instead of her father. Jesse swallowed. He hadn't noticed her appearance when he'd passed by her earlier in the day. She wore a bright green dress, one that brought out the emerald in her eyes and contrasted with her long dark hair, tumbling in soft waves. He ignored the itching to run his fingers through it.

Instead, he pulled the letter out of his pocket. After straightening it out, he shoved it in her hand. "I need to speak to Preston. Does your father know where he is?"

She gasped as she read the contents. A pretty flush spread over her cheeks. "I gave him the day off. He said he needed a day of rest, and I thought… there was no reason to suspect him."

He cursed under his breath.

"I apologize." Evelyn handed the letter back to him. "I had no idea he was planning to see Loretta."

"Do you have any idea where he might be?"

"He said something about riding to the next town over… Harleigh."

He gritted his teeth. Harleigh was larger than Hamilton. She could be anywhere.

Still, it was a better lead than none. He turned to walk back to his horse, until he felt a small hand grip around his wrist. The door locked and footsteps trailed behind him. Evelyn stood in front of him, finally letting go of his wrist.

"I am coming, too. I may not be fit enough for ranch work at the moment, but I can walk on my ankle." Her hands were on her hips and her legs were spread the same width apart as her shoulders. She looked so determined, Jesse expected her to stamp her foot against the floorboards.

"This isn't your concern. I don't want to drag you into this." He looked down at the letter, finally admitting the truth to himself. "It's my fault she ran away."

"Nonsense." Her voice remained firm. It was the same tone she used to boss the other ranch hands around. "Preston works for my father's ranch. If anything goes amiss, we are responsible, too."

"I can't believe he would do something like this." He shook his head. Preston had been one of his good friends since he arrived at the ranch as a boy. How could he betray him by running away with his sister?

"It was probably more of Loretta's doing than his own," Evelyn added. "We will keep this scandal to just the two of us. I will not let any of the other ranch hands know. But if both of us go after them, we might be able to find them faster."

He looked up and met her determined gaze. "All right. Saddle up."

Harleigh ended up being farther than Jesse anticipated. Or at least the town felt like a million miles away, because each second that ticked by without him finding her was another moment his sister could end up eloping and invoking the talk of a whole town. He urged his horse into a gallop as soon as they'd hit the open road. Evelyn kept up with his pace with ease, even sprinted faster than him for most of the ride.

When he and Evelyn finally stepped off their horses, Jesse pointed in the direction of Harleigh's general store. The building was nearly twice the size of the general goods store in Hamilton. "I'll ask the manager if he's seen 'em."

She followed him into the store, her footsteps matching his own against the polished oak floor. Numerous stacks of expensive flour and piles of colorful cotton shirts were strewn every which way. For a store so massive, the customers divided in only a few aisles and gave the store a generally empty look.

The general store manager waited behind one of the desks for customers to purchase goods. He smiled when he first saw Jesse and her, but quickly furrowed his brow when he noticed they were holding nothing for purchase.

"I want to know if you've seen a blond girl and a dark-haired man pass by here. They're from Hamilton, so you might not have seen 'em before today." Jesse took out a tintype of Loretta that he kept in his wallet. He smoothed out the likeness and placed it on the counter. "This is the girl. A little over five feet in height, curly blond hair…"

"Might I interest you in some wonderful calico shirts? They're a rare bargain, I must say. Top-of-the-line quality and at merely half the price you'd find in Hamilton." The manager winked and gestured to the right side of the store. "Or perhaps some fine leather boots with a tough sole for ranch work. You look like a rough fella—"

Evelyn's clipped tone cut him off. "Not interested. Just answer the question."

The manager glared at her but complied with the request. "All right. Well, I ain't never seen the boy you're talking 'bout, but that girl did come in here about an hour ago."

Jesse's heart lifted. "Where did she go afterward? Did she say anything about where she was headed?"

The manager shrugged. "Don't reckon so. How would I know? She didn't even buy that much. Just a few items of stationery, nothing else."

"Which direction did she take when she left the store?" Evelyn pressed, leaning forward.

"Right. She turned right after leaving my store." The manager sighed. "Now if that's all, I must say the beautiful embellished stationery she bought was quite an extraordinary price, such a marvelous bargain, if I may add—"

Evelyn spun around and started walking toward the door before the manager could even finish his sentence. Jesse followed her, resisting the urge to grin. If she hadn't decided to take care of a ranch, she would have made an excellent sheriff.

She stopped outside on the wooden sidewalk, waiting for him. When he caught up to her, she pointed in the direction the manager hinted Loretta had traveled. "What I can't figure out is why Preston wasn't with her. The manager said he only saw Loretta. If they really eloped, where would he be?"

"Maybe he was waiting outside." He started moving, and she marched in step as they scanned the shops.

He entered the saloon, where the bar manager admitted he heard her talking about a tailor. Evelyn dropped into the tailor's, where the man said he thought he saw her go in the direction of the jeweler. Jesse went to the jeweler, who said he'd never seen the girl in his life.

He sat outside the shop, his hat in his hands. The search was proving to be useless. It had been hours since Loretta left her note back at the house. Loretta and Preston could have hightailed it to the next town by now. Maybe there was nothing he could do anymore. Her revenge was finally taking her marriage into her own hands.

Evelyn joined him on the bench. "Why do you look as if you have given up?"

He shrugged. "What's the point? We just keep going in circles, and Loretta's in none of these places."

The wooden bench creaked underneath her added weight. Her honeysuckle scent filled his nostrils. One of her hands rested against his shoulder, and he nearly felt a spark of fire where she touched him. "You cannot give up. Not yet."

Her full lips looked even riper as she scolded him. Jesse ran a hand through his hair. He didn't know which irritated him more, Loretta running off or Evelyn's lips distracting him at every moment.

"I've swallowed my pride at this point, Eve." Her nickname flowed out of his mouth like water before he stopped the leak. She rubbed his back, and waves of comfort washed over him. "I reckon we wouldn't even be here if I had just agreed to let her marry Preston. Then she wouldn't have run away."

"We are not finished searching." Evelyn clucked her tongue. She continued her ministrations, and Jesse wondered if she did this for all her "friends." Her voice was nearly as soft as her touch.

"Give her a chance. Maybe she can explain herself when we find her."

"Explain what? That I was forcing her into a marriage she didn't want?" He spit at the ground. She flinched and dropped her hand from his back. "I thought eventually she'd like him. He's a nice enough fella. He's always wanted to court her."

"What about him is better than Preston?"

"He's from a good family. Loretta would never get that social status otherwise."

"Since when have you been concerned with social status?"

He scowled. "I'm concerned for Loretta, that's all. I care about her."

"So does Preston."

His mouth felt dry suddenly. Preston had probably wanted to court Loretta longer than the doctor's son did, in fact. "He's just a cowboy."

"So were you when I wanted to marry you. When did you change your mind?"

His head jerked sharply at her words. She stared back at him, both a look of sincerity and a challenge in her eyes. There were no traces of remorse for what she'd said.

"The same time you changed yours. Wasn't me being just a cowboy the reason you broke it off between us?"

"I think I made a mistake." Evelyn's lower lip quivered. The fierceness in her green eyes contrasted the tremble in her quiet voice. "I realized that, you know, when you left. I made a mistake by not choosing to marry you."

Jesse was silent, his mind churning.

She laughed, but it had a bitter ring to it. "Say something."

"You could have stopped me." His voice was rough. His head swam with the alternate futures for them if she hadn't chosen to shut him out. Unspoken words coated his throat. "We could have gone to California together."

"What can I do about the past, Jesse? What can I do to apologize?" Her eyes were round, studying his reaction to her words. She pursed her lips, as if considering the possibilities with him. "How can I change what has already happened? The past is behind me."

He wasn't sure how to respond. Putting the past behind her equaled moving on from him, didn't it? But just how much had she forgotten?

"Besides, we have finally become friends again." Her lower lip quivered, the way she did when she was nervous. Her green eyes swam with hope. "That is what we are, right? We are friends."

He felt the stinging burn of the word like a branding iron. Friends. What had once seemed like too much to hope for with Evelyn now didn't seem like enough. It was like she was lassoing him into a title. He tried to wait for the right moment to shuck off the rope, to get beyond being her friend. The longer he waited, the harder it was to escape.

"Reckon so. We're friends." Jesse shifted his weight on the bench. He never heard a word so cursed in all his life. *Friends.* That was all Evelyn saw him as; that was all she'd ever see him as.

"Good. I was worried you were trying to ignore me lately." She managed a small smile, but he caught the tremble in her voice, as if she still didn't believe his words. "There is no reason we should let the past define our present relationships."

"Agreed."

She cleared her throat. "Loretta may not be making a mistake after all. She may be making the right choice."

"How do you figure that?"

"She does not have to wonder, years later, what her life would have been like if she'd just married the cowboy in the first place. She is not letting her fear hold her back." Evelyn licked her lips, and his eyes fell to them.

His gut clenched with regret at his action. Her lips were as red as freshly picked strawberries. Was that what they tasted like?

"I know if the town gets hold of the news, she may be the subject of gossip. But maybe not all the consequences are terrible. Loose talk never lasts for a lifetime. At least she and Preston will not be making the same mistake we did."

He could barely believe the words he was hearing. She regretted it? "Mistake?" He furrowed his brow. His throat felt like gravel, as if the words had difficulty reaching his mouth. "Eve, you wish you'd come to California with me?"

She smiled. There was a sadness to the upward curve of her lips, and moisture pricked the ends of her eyes. "How can I change the past? I think I would have, Jesse. I think I would have followed you anywhere."

She leaned closer as she said the words. Her head tilted, and her lips parted slightly. He felt his whole body lean toward her, like a bear to honey. Their lips edged closer and closer to one another's, until the scent of her enveloped him. He opened his eyes at the last moment, taking in the sight of her beauty before him.

But his eyes narrowed at a shape behind her. He'd seen him before. Cowboy hat, familiar faded red trousers, stained wool shirt—

Wait, was that—?

"Preston!" He stood up, calling his friend's name again. "Preston Dean, get over here!"

# CHAPTER EIGHT

Evelyn nearly fell onto the bench after Jesse stood up. Every time he used her old nickname, her heart started beating faster at the familiarity. Still, discontent prodded her heart. She'd been so sure he was going in for a kiss. Her lips still tingled with the aftereffect, as if her body was physically aware of what should have happened moments ago.

She shook away all romantic notions. They needed to find Loretta first.

Jesse walked down the steps and strode over to Preston. To Evelyn's alarm, he picked up Preston by his coat lapels and shoved him hard against the nearest wall. She ran toward them.

Preston seemed to be waving his hands in defense. "I swear! I did nothing to encourage her! She suggested we come to Harleigh, and then she started talking about eloping once we got here."

"She gave you no warning about running away for good?"

"I swear she didn't!" Preston kept flailing his arms, as if it would wave away Jesse's anger.

"You should have known not to indulge her." He stared daggers at Preston and pulled him up still higher by the lapels. "If you really love her as you say you do—"

"Enough!" Evelyn raised her hand to rest on one of Jesse's arms. He resisted at first, but slowly lowered his grip until Preston's two feet were standing back on the ground.

She turned to Preston and placed her hands on her hips. "Where is Loretta now?"

Preston shook his head. "She ran away from me as soon as I told her we shouldn't elope." He snuck a cautious look at Jesse. "I know it'll ruin her. She got angry at that, though, said her brother had got to me, and just took off."

Jesse's glare didn't ease up. She had never seen him so angry before. "You let her go?" he seethed.

"I've been looking for her this entire time," Preston declared. "I don't plan to leave Harleigh till I find her."

Jesse's scowl remained. Still, he unclenched his fists, Evelyn noted with some relief. "Until we find Loretta, I'm not letting you outta my sight."

Preston turned to her, his eyes searching for a speck of sympathy. "Trust me, I know now that coming here with her was foolish. I figured I'd spend one last day with her before she was married to someone else, that's all."

Evelyn placed her hands on Preston's arms and shushed him. "You need to help us find Loretta. That would be mighty appreciated."

"You believe me, don't you?"

"I believe you." She winced. "I cannot say Jesse does, though."

Jesse had already started walking down the long line of stores by the time she turned around. She ran after him and grabbed his wrist to stop him. This time he shrugged her off. She nearly tripped backward, taken aback by his sudden jerk of her hand.

"We are trying to help you."

"How? Now that we've found Preston, we have no idea where she is. How can you help?" he snapped.

Evelyn narrowed her eyes at him. "Loretta is my friend, too. And she considers Preston her sweetheart, whether you like it or not. We do not like this situation any more than you do."

"What's your great idea, hmm?" He scuffed one of his boots against the dirt, causing a plume of dust to rise up. "Think we can just keep jawing and standing around and my sister will just show up outta nowhere?"

"No, I think we will keep talking and reason this situation out." She scowled. "You were always all action. You never actually think through a situation, do you? This is not Preston's fault. He wants Loretta found and safe as much as you do."

His jaw tensed as he saw Preston catch up to them. Still, she believed her words had some effect on him. He wasn't glaring at Preston anymore. That was progress.

"Where was the last place you saw her?"

Preston pointed to outside the nearest hotel. "She was trying to convince me to stay there with her. I refused. You know me. She just gave her words a lick and a promise. I said she was going to be married, that it wasn't proper."

"Then?"

"She ran on into the hotel before I could stop her."

Jesse folded his arms over his chest. "Why didn't you go in after her?"

"Well, I did, but by then no one was in there. The hotel clerk was gone, and I waited for a while but no one came. I gave up and figured she'd be back out here in the town."

"That's all?"

"What else could I have done?"

"You check every room in that hotel," Jesse muttered.

"Doesn't make any sense to me. She's probably out here in this town."

Jesse's right hand twitched, as if resisting the urge to clench into a fist and deal a blow. Her eyes widened when she noticed and quickly set her hands on his folded arms. "We will all just look at this situation without being hasty." She turned to Preston. "If you think she is here in the town, where might she be? Did she have any reason for choosing Harleigh?"

"Said she wanted to buy some things from the general store, but I already checked that place."

"We're never going to find her here." Jesse rubbed the back of his neck. His eyes scanned the maze of stores of the town with a dismissive eye. "Lord knows she could be anywhere by now."

Preston's eyes lit up. "Lord knows." He kept repeating the phrase over and over, like a strange prayer of some sort. "Lord knows, that's it! The Lord knows!"

Evelyn bent her head toward Preston's, eyebrows raised. "The Lord knows what?"

Preston Dean grinned. "I think I know where she is."

• • •

Jesse watched his sister for a few seconds, kneeling at the altar of the church. Her fingers were laced tightly together, and her elbows rested on the wooden pedestal in front of her. His sister's hair fell in two long plaits down her white summer dress. Her closed eyes and wavy blond tendrils framing her face made her appear nearly angelic. She looked as innocent as a young girl in a small Texan town could ever be.

He knew otherwise.

"Loretta Greenwood, you are in trouble."

Her eyes snapped open. She stood up in a flash, her hands unclasped and all thoughts of prayer forgotten. "How did you find me?" Her lower lip quivered.

"Preston told us. Evelyn's waiting with him outside." Jesse jerked a thumb over his shoulder. "He told us you might be here."

"Evelyn? How did she find out?" Loretta turned her eyes downward. "Not that it matters. She understands I love Preston. Unlike you."

He sighed. "No, I didn't understand. But I do know that this is never going to happen again."

She gulped. With the backs of her hands, she swiped away the tears beginning to fall down her cheeks. "You must think me some great fool. He didn't even want to elope. Said it would ruin me and you'd die of the worry—"

"I nearly did." He furrowed his brow. "Don't ever scare me like that again, Loretta."

"This is the place, isn't it?" A sob wracked her chest. Loretta gestured to the pews and the main aisle of the Harleigh church. "This is where I am going to be married."

"Yes, yes, it is." He walked toward his sister and pointed to the altar. "This is where the preacher will stand as the wedding takes place. Then outside…" His index finger moved from the front of the church to the back door. "Outside is where the supper will be afterward, and everyone from the ranch is invited."

Her eyes remained downcast. "Even Preston?"

Jesse cleared his throat. "Oh, I should reckon so. The wedding can't happen without him."

"What?"

He looked up at the rafters in a nonchalant manner. "Last time I checked, a wedding can't happen without the groom." He glanced back at Loretta, who grinned from ear to ear.

"You don't say! Oh, you don't say!" Loretta ran up to him and threw her arms around her older brother. He stiffened at first, then patted her back. When she pulled away, the sides of her eyes were still moist. He was afraid she'd burst out crying again. "I can finally marry Preston?"

"I shouldn't have stopped you in the first place. Clearly, if you're willing to risk your reputation to run away and to elope with him…" His voice trailed off as a sudden memory entered his mind. He swallowed hard. "Then clearly this is beyond my interference. You marry who you want, Loretta."

"Oh thank you! Thank you, thank you!" Loretta jumped up and down with childlike enthusiasm. He smiled in spite of himself. She turned to the door in a hesitant way, as if checking for affirmation from her brother again.

"Go on," he encouraged.

She didn't need to be told twice. He watched her run toward the door, throw open the entrance, and squeal as she jumped into Preston's waiting arms. Preston twirled her around the end of the church aisle, then grabbed her hand and guided her away from the church. Their voices drifted off as he heard them talk animatedly about future plans and living arrangements.

Once Preston and Loretta had passed from the door, he watched Evelyn walk up the length of the aisle. He still stood at the altar, rooted in place, as his gaze locked with hers. Even though she stood at the end of the pews, he could hear her approval.

"Loretta's beyond my control at this point." He started to walk forward, mimicking her motion as the two of them strolled toward the center of the aisle.

"No regrets?" His heart skipped as Evelyn's smile broke into a grin.

"None."

"You made the right choice. Loretta will be happy with Preston." Her green eyes sparkled at her small victory. "You listened to me, after all."

"Wouldn't have a lick of difference. No matter what I say to her, my sister has a will of her own."

"Still. Preston would not have agreed to marry her without your approval."

"True. At least one of them has some sense."

"She is too young for proper sense, Jesse. Give her time." She had nearly reached him now, just a few feet away. "You were her age once."

"Didn't have much sense then, did I?"

Evelyn laughed, and the sound sent a thrill up his spine. He was surprised to discover he would still do anything to hear her laugh again. "Neither of us did."

"I seem to remember possessing more sense than you."

"That's strange. Reckon it was the other way around. I might need proof."

"I can refresh your memory, if you would prefer." Her teasing smile made his stomach tighten.

He and Evelyn stood less than a foot apart. Her honeysuckle scent permeated the air between them, the familiarity nearly overwhelming him with its sinister sweetness. Silence fell between the both of them.

She lifted her hand to grasp his.

"Evelyn!"

Her hand dropped from his.

The call hadn't come from Jesse. It came from the end of the aisle.

She spun around. She dropped his hand and pressed both of her arms against her sides. His palm still tingled where she'd touched him.

He watched John Cooper stride up the aisle. *Glide* was a better description. His coat looked more like a cape, and his shoes created a clipping sound against the wooden floorboards. The paleness of his cheeks made Jesse wonder if the judge's son had ever spent a day outdoors doing physical labor. He doubted John Cooper ever would.

He gritted his teeth when John stopped at Evelyn's side. He slipped his hand into hers—freely, openly, as if it was the most natural thing in the world. She flinched at first, but she didn't pull away.

The sight made Jesse want to vomit.

"Evelyn, you have not introduced me to all your friends." John stuck out his free hand. "I am John Cooper, the judge's son."

He stared at the hand instead. Even John's palm was white as a ghost's, contrasting Jesse's own deep tan from days under the sun.

John looked down at his lonely, outstretched gesture, then tucked his hand away into his pocket as if he'd never offered it.

"Well." John tried to meet Evelyn's eyes, but hers were averted to the floor. "Pleasure to meet you, Mister…"

"Greenwood. Jesse Greenwood." He inclined his head toward John. "I'm one of the ranch hands at Breighton."

"He has truly helped the ranch to recover again," Evelyn added. Any small surge of pride Jesse had felt at her compliment was quickly squashed when John squeezed Evelyn's hand.

"Of course. Anyone helps my sweetheart is a friend of mine." John flashed him that white-toothed grin he hated so much.

*Sweetheart?*

Jesse didn't realize he'd asked the question out loud until John answered. "She has given me permission to court her, Mr. Greenwood." John gave her a look as adoring as it was horrifying. "My persistence seems to have paid off. She is the only one I have wanted to marry since I laid my eyes on her."

"John, stop." Evelyn's voice had an edge to it.

"Why, I can show you off if I like. I do not deserve you, and I do not care who knows it."

The only thing Jesse deserved was to wake up from the terrible dream. But Evelyn wasn't protesting. She just tensed her shoulders at John's words. *Probably because she doesn't want to hurt my feelings.* She grabbed men's hands out of friendship. The near-kiss had only existed in his imagination.

What wasn't confined to his imagination, though, was John Cooper turning away from Jesse with Evelyn's arm looped around his. She looked over her shoulder as she moved down the aisle with John. Her expression seemed to be apologizing.

Jesse swallowed hard. To think he'd actually believed she cared for him.

# CHAPTER NINE

"Is there something wrong?"

Yes. Yes, everything was wrong. Nothing was right. The man whom she thought she loved had let her walk away despite her repeated attempts to hold his hand and talk to him.

The man who did love her and wrote her letters of affection blinked back at her from across the restaurant table. She refocused her vision on John and smiled. "Yes, yes, of course everything is simply fine." As if the action could disguise her lie, she brushed a lock of dark hair behind her ear. "I was just thinking about the ranch. Nothing else."

John's eyes clouded over with understanding. Or, as much as a man who'd spent his entire life indoors and out of business could wrap his mind around worrying about a ranch. "I understand the farm is doing much better. How is your father, by the way? Is he still ill?"

"He seems to be doing better now, thank you," she replied for the fifteenth time.

"That is wonderful news."

She resisted the urge to roll her eyes. "I told you so yesterday." *And you said the same response yesterday as well.*

"Yes, well, his status could have changed. He could have taken a turn for the worse." John patted his hand on hers.

She drew her hand away. The same way Jesse had recoiled from her touch when she'd tried to hold his hand the first time.

John waved his hand, dismissing the topic. "Did you know San Francisco uses a cable car now? Imagine! Just think of a cable car in every city."

Evelyn couldn't have cared less about cable cars, or about anything John Cooper ever had to say. There was such a contrast between him and Jesse. While she and Jesse could settle into comfortable silences, John seemed to hurry to fill all the quiet moments with conversation, as if talking about rubbish would deepen their relationship.

She ignored the slight ache in her chest when she thought of Jesse. He'd been ignoring her again ever since he'd talked to John in the church. He didn't even go out of his way to avoid her, like he had before. This time it was just polite hellos and good evenings, which was even worse.

She found herself drifting out of the conversation. By the time she realized John was still speaking, she had no idea where his turn of conversation had come from.

"When we are married and live at my house, of course, we should have a telegraph in the parlor…"

Marriage?

Evelyn managed a tight smile, her endurance flagging. "You have put a lot of thought into these plans. But surely it is too early in our courtship to talk of our married life."

John leaned forward so much that she was afraid he would knock over his bowl and spill his mutton stew all over the table. "When can we talk about it, Evelyn?"

She grabbed her glass of water and took a long sip from it, as if gulping would give the answer to his question. The idea of marrying John filled her heart with unease. Why was he so insistent?

"Surely you must understand how I care for you. You plan to live the remainder of your life alone and die all by yourself with no one else around you?"

Goodness, she had never considered being single that way. She set down the glass. "Someday, I suppose I will—"

He clapped his hands together as if the matter were already settled. "Then I will do everything within my power to convince you of marriage as soon as possible. You will love married life."

Her shoulders sagged. His optimism made her want to agree with him. She struggled to find solace in the idea of a future with John. He did love her, after all. He'd sent the letters. She turned toward him. "I miss the letters. You have stopped sending them."

He coughed. "Why would I? They no longer appear necessary now, my dear."

She shot him a quizzical expression. He shifted in his seat. Why did John look so uncomfortable all of a sudden?

"Those letters were to help me get close to you, dearest Evelyn." John placed a hand over his heart. "I was expressing my honest feelings for you."

She wished he would stop giving her endearments. "But surely you could leave another letter again, even if we are courting formally."

"Is there another man?"

She blinked. An image of Jesse flashed through her mind. "What?"

"There is another man, is there not? Another man you prefer over me?"

"I… I do not know what you are talking about."

"I am handsome, brave, and wealthy. But that seems to not be enough for you. You seem to want me to prove my feelings for you further. Am I competing against someone?" John lifted a brow. He clasped his hands over his bowl, elbows propped up on the table.

She remained silent, and he sighed. "Has he asked to court you as well?"

"No, no, he has not." Her mouth felt dry. "I was under the delusion that he cared for me, but I do not think so anymore."

He clucked his tongue. "This gentleman is missing out on a wonderful woman. Did he ever express his feelings for you?"

"Once. A long time ago." Memories of a brown-haired cowboy drifted to the top of her mind.

"Does he still feel the same way?"

"No, he does not."

John placed his palms on the table and sighed again, as if the world was a great mystery to him and he couldn't be bothered with it. "I am deeply humbled that he would forsake such a beautiful treasure for me, a simple man."

Evelyn nearly rolled her eyes again at his theatrics. "No one is competing with you."

"How he ever gave up on you, I shall never understand."

She bit her lower lip. Had Jesse given up on her? He had never shown romantic interest in her, really. He'd never kissed her, never reached to hold her hand… never wrote the letters.

The letters were what she missed above all. Even if the notes did not come from him, the words were so genuine and touching. There were no theatrics or polish. It was odd, really, that John's written words were so wonderful and simple, yet his spoken words seemed meaningless and empty.

No one loved her as much as the author of the letters. Evelyn tried to shake off the unsettling feeling in her chest. She had to face the facts—John Cooper had written the letters, and not Jesse Greenwood.

John lifted his glass. "May I propose a toast?"

"To what?"

He eyes softened. "To the beginning of our relationship."

She always imagined when she'd finally heard those words, she'd feel a sense of joy and excitement. But John's words only made her wish she was back at Breighton instead of sitting in the restaurant with him. Evelyn snapped out of her reverie when she felt John's hand cover hers again. There was no comfort in the gesture, like when she'd held hands with Jesse in the church.

There was only a dull weight over her palm, and a sinking feeling in her heart.

• • •

Jesse ran through the list one more time with the general store manager, checking to make sure everything had been ordered for the wedding. He didn't understand why she couldn't send one of her friends down to the store instead, but Loretta had insisted she trusted only him to make sure everything on the list was taken care of.

He figured she'd probably done so partly out of guilt, since he was paying for all the items. She'd assured him before he left that if there was anything on the list that was too expensive, he did not have to place the order. After checking the purchases twice, he folded the list into his pocket. She still didn't seem to register that money wasn't an obstacle anymore.

As he walked away, the general store owner called after him that the items would be ready to pick up a day before the wedding. Jesse thanked him, and opened the doors of the store—bumping into a woman passing along the street. Her packages fell, tumbling to the floorboards with a clatter. Guilt wracked his chest. He kneeled down to help her.

"Oh, it's quite all right, I'll be just fine..." The woman's voice trailed off, and her hands stilled over one of the packages.

Jesse looked up at the familiar redhead. He inclined the tall crown of his hat toward her. "Hello, Annie."

Annie Inglewood looked like she'd just seen a ghost. He'd never really known her growing up; he only knew her as Evelyn's friend now. The few times he had seen her growing up, she'd never looked this surprised. Her jaw dropped, and her blue eyes bored straight into his. He placed the last package into her hands, but her limp arm barely held it as she continued to stare.

He stood, and she did the same. Suddenly she didn't look so shocked anymore. Her chapped lips curved into a smile, and she seemed to be blinking faster than normal.

"Is there something in your eye?" He pointed to her eye but dropped his hand when the blinking stopped.

"Oh no, I was just batting my lashes at the handsomest man who entered Hamilton." Annie's eyes shined like a proud cowboy who'd just caught a wild white mustang. "Jesse Greenwood, I heard you were back in town. But no one sure told me how handsome you've become."

He shifted his weight on the wooden floorboards. No one had ever called him handsome. "Handsome" was a word that belonged to men from blue-blooded families, not rugged ranch hands. He wasn't sure what to do with the flattery. "Thank you, Miss Inglewood. Now if you'll excuse me…"

He moved to walk around her right side. But she stepped to her left, blocking his path. "I hear you're in town for your sister's wedding." A bright red blush rushed to her cheeks as she continued. "Evelyn mentioned to me that you were working back on the ranch. You must miss being further west. It must be so exciting out there in California. You've become quite the self-made man."

"Just a man, no different than anyone else."

"Hardly. She told me about your investment. You're the rags to riches cowboy. I bet if people in Hamilton knew what you've done for the ranch, they would all be beside themselves gossiping about you."

He didn't want to be the subject of gossip in the town. He wanted to get back to his ranch. "I think I will be heading back after my sister marries. Breighton's barn has been fixed. I've made my investment and seen it through. I won't be needed much longer."

"Oh, of course. I'm sure after the wedding John will help out around the ranch as well."

Jesse smirked. He sincerely doubted John knew what a corral was, much less know how to build one. Then the realization of her words sank in. "Wedding?" There was no way he was staying in town for Evelyn's marriage.

Annie nodded. She leaned in closer to his ear, as if she was whispering a secret with the power of changing the fate of the entire state of Texas. "I shouldn't be telling you this, but I heard him bragging to his father that within the year he was going to marry her, come hell or high water." She flipped a curl behind her shoulder. "For them, marriage is just a step away. Everyone says John's wanted to marry her since he set eyes on her. Surely you must know."

He did know. He'd have to be blind not to. Every afternoon he saw John Cooper's horse hitched in front of the big house at Breighton. Sometimes John wouldn't leave until evening, with Evelyn watching his horse ride away from the porch.

Jesse caught her eyes a few times, but he didn't dare delude himself any longer. She had chosen John Cooper.

"How are you and Evelyn?" Annie tilted her head, batting her thick lashes once more. "I know you two used to be sweet on each other, but that was ages ago." Her eyes seemed to grow alarmingly larger as the seconds ticked by, waiting for his confirmation. "You don't care for her anymore, do you?"

He flicked his gaze away from Annie and shrugged. She was as prying as Loretta. "Reckon not. Why would I be sweet on a girl who's chosen to court another fella?" He asked himself that question every morning. Why was he, anyway?

"Good," Annie responded a little too quickly. She seemed to realize it, too, because she covered her mouth after the word slipped out.

"Just life. Time changes everything."

"First love is not the last love. That's what my mother is always telling me. I think she's right."

No, Jesse wanted to add, it could be the only love. He kept quiet instead, as he saw Evelyn and John approaching them.

John's grip around her arm tightened as they slowed to a halt in front of Annie and Jesse. Jesse's hands twitched in reflex. His every instinct wanted to grab John's hand and wrench it away from her.

"Evelyn, what a pleasure to see you!" Annie threw her arms around her friend. When she pulled away, she giggled. "I see you and John have been getting along."

John patted Evelyn's hand. "And it is always a pleasure to see you again, Annie. Jesse, how is your sister's wedding coming along?"

"Fine."

John raised his eyebrow. "And how is Loretta?"

"Fine."

He laughed. "Is that the only word you know?"

She elbowed him, and he scowled. His grip clenched her tighter.

The urge to yank John's arm away from Evelyn's was stronger than ever. He hated the way John handled her. Now that she'd finally agreed to let him court her, he acted as if he owned her. How could she spend time with a man who treated her like cattle? "Both of you are invited to her wedding. She sent out the letters today."

"Of course, I will be happy to come." Evelyn smiled at Jesse. She unhooked John's arm from hers, and Jesse suppressed a grin when she glared at the other man. "Do not grab me, John."

"*We* will be happy to come." John remained undeterred in his mission to brand Evelyn as his own. The judge's son draped an arm around her, and Jesse's insides churned again. "Will we not, dearest Evelyn?"

She dropped her gaze from Jesse's, as if ashamed. "Yes, Father is coming with some of the other ranch hands. John is taking me in his buggy down to the church."

He raised an eyebrow at Jesse. "Are you traveling to the wedding by yourself?" He looked him up and down, his pleasant tone disguising a patronizing gaze.

He didn't know what possessed him just then. He clenched his fists, though he knew he couldn't lay a blow so long as Evelyn stood there. She'd never forgive him. But after seeing another man's arm slung across her shoulder as if he owned her, hearing Evelyn admit she was allowing John to accompany her to Loretta's wedding—something inside him snapped.

"Annie's accompanying me." Jesse watched with a sick sense of satisfaction as John's eyes widened in surprise. He couldn't bring himself to look at Evelyn.

Annie didn't miss a beat. If she'd been caught off guard, she sure didn't show it. "I said yes immediately, of course. The wedding will be just grand." She did that fast blinking that Jesse vaguely understood to be flirtatious. "Couldn't let the most handsome man in Hamilton walk away, now, could I?"

"Well, then!" John clapped a hand on Jesse's shoulder. He tensed at the contact. "Seems like we have both managed to find ourselves our own pretty women to court."

"Seems like we have." Another flare of jealousy rose within him when John called Evelyn *his*. She wasn't a possession. "Cannot wait to see you at the wedding."

"Evelyn, we must get ready together. We simply must," Annie gushed. She hooked her arm around Jesse's. "I would not miss the event for the entire world."

Evelyn remained quiet. She only nodded at Annie's comment, as if her mind were already preoccupied with something else. Probably financial matters on the ranch.

· · ·

Evelyn wanted to leave. She tugged on John's arm and told him so, and then they said their goodbyes and started back toward Breighton. He insisted on accompanying her back to the house, but she managed to convince him she was tired and needed rest.

The moment his horse disappeared at the end of the road, she'd left for the stables to clear her head with an evening ride.

She hadn't even had enough courage to look Jesse in the eye. She didn't know why her chest ached when she thought of Jesse and Annie together. If he really didn't care for her and Annie was the one he wanted, then she was just being selfish.

Not to mention disloyal. She was supposed to be falling for John, not Jesse. She'd practically sealed her fate to him when she'd allowed him to court her.

Evelyn pressed her upper body closer to Blue Star, urging her horse forward into a gallop back to the house. All she wanted was a warm bed and a respite from courtship of any kind. Jesse was older than she: twenty-four. He was more than old enough to begin courting a woman. He could be married with children by now.

He'd never truly courted Evelyn, not in the proper way that society encouraged. She somehow doubted sneaking out to the stables after sunset was proper.

How had John known Jesse was interested in Annie, anyway? She wrinkled her nose. Grabbing her arm like that, as if she was his dog and he was trying to discipline her. She shook her head. Surely a man who wrote such affectionate letters would never intend to hurt her. He was just upset she elbowed him, that's all.

She spent the rest of the day in bed, poring over all the letters she'd received. Some of the writing along the creased lines had faded from the amount of times she had folded and unfolded the letters. She knew at least half of them by heart.

The lines were read by the last light of the sun as it set beyond the plains once she'd brought them out to the porch. She set aside half of the stack when another envelope caught her eye—a new letter, nestled between the posts.

Evelyn rubbed her eyes to make sure she wasn't seeing visions. No, the envelope still lay against the column, her name written in the same scribbled scrawl she had come to love. It looked just like the others, but kept on the porch instead of its usual knothole.

She picked it up and tore open the seal. The letter fell into her lap, waiting to be read. The penmanship was the same as the other letters, but messier, as if written in a hurry. Could it be John apologizing?

Dearest love,

I don't know what's come over me these days. Letting you go has been one of the hardest things I've ever done. I'm not giving you up—but what can I do? If you want someone else, it's not in my power to stop you. I thought maybe if I let you go, then I'd stop loving you. It couldn't be farther from the truth, and that's dawned on me now. Maybe my love for you means I allow you to love who you want. Loving someone means letting that person go.

Evelyn folded the letter and placed it back into the envelope. Letting her go? She had just seen John; she hadn't let him go at all. Her brows furrowed. Well, she had mentioned that there was another man she'd wanted first. Maybe that was whom John was referring to.

A small surge of satisfaction filled her as she walked back into the house and toward her desk. John had listened to her request and written another letter. She sat down and pulled out a sheet of paper. The letter deserved a reply, even if it wasn't from Jesse.

• • •

There was something to a Texan sunset.

The ones in California were gorgeous, of course, with rich hues of purple and blue tinting the sky. But he'd felt there was something missing every time he looked at it. Whatever was incomplete became whole when he saw the sunset in Texas again.

Maybe it was the memories. The memories of holding Evelyn against him while they watched the sunset together, admiring the red sun dip its head below the end of the prairie, farther than the eye could see and beyond the borders of the ranch. Maybe it was the shadows. The shadows of seeing the profile of a cowboy on his horse in the distance, a lone rider admiring the sunset in solitude. The shadows of home.

Jesse leaned against the top railing of the corral, his arms folded over the top. The cool Texan wind blew against the back of his neck, causing the hairs to stand. Either that, or Evelyn's voice behind him.

"The sunset is beautiful, is it not?"

"Sure is." He adjusted his hat on the top of his head, refusing to look behind him.

But he didn't need to. She stood next to him, leaning against the top railing as well.

He couldn't help it. His eyes averted to the left, watching her close her eyes and breathe in deep in the direction of the sunset.

His heart lurched. Her hair was done up in some fancy style, but loose tendrils dropped from the bun, falling down along the nape of her neck. She smiled against the wind as her eyes closed, enjoying the night air around her. When her eyes flashed back open to see the sunset, he looked away.

"Do you remember watching these sunsets together?"

"Not really." Lies. How could he forget? He tensed his jaw. What good would it do to tell her he thought about it all the time?

"I think about it. I think about it a lot, really." She laughed, but the sound was hoarse and devoid of joy. "That first year after you left for California, I watched the sunset every night. I used to imagine that cowboy in the distance was you, riding back here to Breighton..." Her voice trailed off.

"That was a long time ago." He cleared his throat. He felt at war between inhaling that sweet honeysuckle scent and pushing her away. She'd chosen another man over him. She was off limits, he reminded himself. "We were just kids."

"At the time we thought we were so grown up." Her voice sounded thoughtful as she considered the past. Not thoughtful; she sounded dangerous. Remembering the past led to nothing but heartbreak. "Reckon I was a lot poorer and a lot more foolish."

She spun to face him. The corners of her eyes were soft, as if she didn't want to be misunderstood. "No, that is not what I mean at all. We just acted like we had nothing to lose. Nothing could get in our way."

"Don't know why I acted that way." He turned his head and clasped his hands over the railing. "It doesn't matter what you mean. That's in the past now."

"It still matters." He'd never heard a voice more firm and stubborn than Evelyn Lancaster's. "And why do you call me Evelyn? What happened to calling me 'Eve' again?"

He swallowed hard. He hadn't even dared to use her nickname, afraid of being consumed by the absoluteness of the word. He'd only used it out of affection. He'd only used it when there was a hope of a future together.

"We are friends, Jesse." Evelyn pressed her hand against his arm. The dreaded word rose once more. He tensed, and then she let go. "Friends confide in each other. I miss talking to you openly. I feel like you are hiding some matter from me." She paused. "Is there something you wish to tell me?"

He mumbled something under his breath.

"What?" She narrowed her eyes, leaning closer to him to hear what he said.

"*Imisswhenyouweremine.*" He looked down at the dirt. Had he really just said it out loud?

Evelyn stepped back. Her eyes were wide. Clearly she'd heard him. He steeled himself for her refusal, for her rejection of him again. He'd suffered it once. He thought he could do it again.

"I miss you, too."

His heart beat fast. Fear gripped his heart at the first sign of hope. Dangerous hope, that's what it was.

Jesse lifted his head to catch her gaze. She stood there, her hands still draped over the railing, staring right back at him with those soft green orbs of hers, which clean took his breath away.

"I have missed you since I told you we could not be together. That day when I went to the bunkhouse to see you…" The corner of her strawberry-red lips quirked upward. "I think I went there so soon after I returned because I was terrified. I worried otherwise I would give in to my own emotions and not have the courage to turn you away."

It blew him away how much tenderness could exist in Evelyn's gaze. The feeling inside Jesse was nearly more than he could take. He wanted to spend all his time with this girl. He wanted her by his side forever. The desire terrified him.

She still waited for his reply. "Is there anything else you want to say, Jesse?"

Suddenly irritation flared inside him. She couldn't keep him in a constant state of confusion. Here she was, grabbing his hand and jawing love confessions, but her actions proved otherwise. She was on the fast track to a marriage with the judge's son, for Christ's sake. "Why are you courting that John Cooper fella?"

"He is a good man. I have never met anyone quite so honest." She blushed. "He asked to court me. You never asked."

What if I'd asked, his lips itched to say. *What if I'd stepped in before he did?* But he kept quiet. There was no point in arguing. As far as he knew, Cooper could be as honest as scripture and never told a lie in his life. "Doesn't seem like enough to agree to court him, if you ask me."

Evelyn bit her lip. "He is from a good family. The Cooper family has provided a long line of judges to this county for as long as anyone can remember."

"Rich folks, born and bred." Jesse's heart clenched, and his voice came out gruffer than intended. "Never figured you to choose a husband based on social standing."

She gasped. "I did not!"

"Upper class, one of the Coopers. Oldest family in Hamilton. He's as blue-blooded as they get."

"No, I told him he could court me. I chose based on his character…"

"You chose based on status."

"You must be joking!"

"Security. You marry him, then you'll be one of the Coopers and gain all that social standing, too." He watched her gulp as his voice grew louder. "But he's not enough. You wouldn't be here talking with me if he were enough."

"I do not know what you are referring to."

"You're letting him court you so you can marry and dine with upper-class society, and then you think you can come back to me and forget all about him."

"What are you saying?"

"I'm predicting your future. It's as you said. You marry someone else, then you just sneak around with me." Jesse spit at the ground. Women had no right to lead on men they had no intention of marrying. Her behavior wasn't just offensive; it was harmful.

"I'll have nothing to do with this." She stuttered, searching for words. "My life… my life has nothing to do with you!"

He grew bolder, closing the distance between them. "If he means so much to you, why do you always approach me, hmm? If you say we just existed in the past, why do you keep holding me back in the present?"

Her brows furrowed. "Holding? Is that what you believe I am doing? Am I holding you back from living your life now?" She gritted her teeth. "I was extending friendship to you, and all you do is either ignore me or fight with me. John would never do that."

"Admit it. You don't care a continental for Cooper."

"I do!"

"All you care about is keeping your line in the upper class."

"He loves me. He tells me so whenever he comes to the house. He does not insult me." Her chin lifted upward in that proud way of hers. "Unlike others."

"Oh, and I insult you?"

"I never said that."

"You barely know him."

"I know he has never done anything to disprove his character. His respectable breeding came before him, but he has lived up to it as an honest man."

He scowled. "You think I don't know I still belong with the ranch hands?" He reached out to place his hands on the railing, spaced on either side of Evelyn's head. She stood there, pinned underneath him, as still as a train track. "New money's never been accepted in this traditional town. It doesn't matter how much wealth I earned in California. I'll never reach the social standing of an old family like Cooper's."

His breath came out in hard puffs of air. Her honeysuckle scent overwhelmed him now.

She overwhelmed him.

She prodded his chest, her index finger jabbing out her anger against him. "You do not insult Breighton and the entire town of Hamilton. You have no right. Just because someone is from an established family does not mean they discriminate."

"Reckon you're lying." He leaned closer, his lips gravitating toward hers.

"I am not!" She stamped her foot. "I do not discriminate!" But as soon as the words left her mouth, the color drained from her face and all the fire faded out.

"Yes, you did." He leaned closer still, until a simple turn of his head would have landed her lips on his. "The reason you rejected me the first time was because I wasn't from your social class."

Her voice became quiet. "I thought I could pursue a career. But then the ranch needed help, and I thought…"

"You thought marrying someone wealthy was your only choice."

Evelyn nibbled her lower lip. "I… I was so young… I was not thinking straight," she managed finally. Her shoulders slumped in a sign of defeat.

He remained silent, his breath mingling with hers as the warm air circulated between their lips. The cold darkness after sunset meant he could see her breath in puffs of air. The cloud of warm breath mixed with the unspoken words floating between them.

"You say you miss me. You say you made a mistake." His voice lowered, barely above a whisper.

"I did miss you."

"But just reckon—just reckon if you could go back to that moment before you ended us, if I'd told you to run away with me to California…"

"We cannot repeat the past, Jesse."

"I'm not asking for a repeat. I'm asking for an answer. Would you have gone with me?"

Silence hung over them like a veil. Her eyes clouded over, making her expression unreadable. Seconds ticked by. With each moment, his anger gave way to acceptance.

Finally, Evelyn tore her eyes away from his and stared down at the laces of her shoes. "I need to go back to the house." She pushed against him to get out of his hold, and he stepped back, dropping his arms at the unexpected contact.

He watched her run back to the house, as far away from him as she could. Her black high-top shoes pattered against the wooden floorboards of her porch as she hurried away.

He started to walk after her, but paused when he passed by the tree. An envelope lay in the tree's knothole, but not his own. The letter he'd written to her was gone, replaced by a new one. He swallowed hard. Probably a letter informing her secret admirer that he had to stop writing to her.

He picked it up, nevertheless, and brought it to his room. He paused in the hallway when he passed by her door, dying to knock and talk to her again. He ignored the urge instead, and picked up his pace to reach the end of the hallway.

As soon as he'd entered his room, he tore open the envelope and set the letter down on the desk. He lit a nearby candle, and read the letter.

Dearest,

I must admit, I still love receiving your letters. You are very bad, indeed, for I am already courting a man named John Cooper. You may know him? Tall, well-spoken, extremely persistent. Of course you know him. You cannot argue with the persistence part I added in there. I think even you would find the description accurate. You, my admirer, seem to look past all my flaws, and for that I am grateful. I am grateful you have started writing to me again. How one would ever think of marrying me, I'll never understand. But I have given you my permission to court me and my permission still stands.

Love,
Evelyn

Jesse furrowed his brow. Permission? She has to be joking, of course.

He dropped the letter on the desk. It didn't matter. The contents of the letter were as he'd feared. She wanted him to stop writing to her. She'd only penned the letter to inform her admirer that she was in love with John Cooper.

His mind drifted back to the image of her slamming the porch door shut behind her. She'd shut the door on him, as well.

# CHAPTER TEN

Annie powdered her nose for the fifteenth time that hour. She scrutinized herself in her vanity, admiring her work. "I swear, the moment Jesse Greenwood walked through that general store door and into my life, I knew it was love."

Evelyn smoothed out her dress, creasing away the wrinkles. Annie would never stop talking about him. "Do not be too hasty to label your feelings as love."

Her friend whirled around and clasped her hands below her chin. She could practically see the stars shining in her eyes.

"I know you two used to carry on a relationship, but that was more than seven years ago, Evelyn. It is all right, isn't it? I know he has not asked to court me *for certain*, but he did suddenly invite me to the wedding as if emotion had seized his throat and his wonderful lips burst out the words his beating heart was dying to express!" Annie flung her arms out, nearly hitting the vanity mirror and causing Evelyn to flinch.

She thought back to his words from the other night. When he'd cornered her against the corral, pinning her beneath him—

Evelyn flushed, and stamped out the inner yearning she felt inside. "We were together so long ago. I'm with John now. If Jesse spends time with you, it is none of my business anymore."

But Annie paid no attention to Evelyn's words. She carried on, preoccupied with her future life. "It's only a hope that he'll court me, of course. But I believe he will. No, I know he will!" Annie's eyes were alight with excitement. "I think he invited me to the wedding today as a precursor of what's to come."

"What's to come?"

"Why, the wedding between Jesse and me, of course! This is a prediction of our own impending marriage."

The years had changed Evelyn, but not Annie Inglewood. She was just as much of a hopeless romantic as she was at sixteen. "I know we do not usually agree on matters, but you should be practical."

"But I am a woman in love! How could I possibly be practical?"

Evelyn smiled in spite of herself. "Wedding, hmm? You never spoke of him like this before he left for California."

"Oh, but haven't you noticed how incredibly *handsome* he's become?" Annie's lips parted, and Evelyn was afraid she would start drooling. "I always thought he was good-looking, but you were with him at the time." Annie unclasped her hands to place them on her cheeks. "I will never flirt with him if you want him. Just say the word, and I will drop all feelings for him without so much as a second glance."

*Then it is not love*, Evelyn wanted to add. *You should not be able to let him go so easily.* "I did not know you were soft on him, even then."

Annie batted her lashes. "I didn't know either. Maybe that's the nature of love. It just emerges all of a sudden and takes you by surprise when you least expect it. You think your life is going one way, you think you're going to settle with someone, and then suddenly love turns your life in a different direction."

Seeing her friend so happy once more gave her joy, even if the cause didn't.

Jesse's words had repeated themselves in her head since he'd said them: *Reckon if you could go back, go back to that moment...*

She'd replayed the scenario like a guitarist who only knew one song. What would she have chosen? Would she have left her home behind?

"Though I must say, I can't imagine Loretta not being with Preston." Annie huffed. "The two are inseparable, always have been. If I were her and being forced to marry someone I didn't love, I'd clean run away!"

"Would you?" She raised a brow in Annie's direction. "You could give up your family and your friends and your home?"

Annie gave her a condescending look, as if Evelyn was an idiot. When she spoke, however, her voice was gentle, emphasizing each word. "No place can be a home without love."

There was a sharp rap from the front door. Annie looked into the vanity one last time before opening the door and smiling at the men on the other side. "Why, Mr. Cooper!" Her voice lowered. "And hello, Mr. Greenwood."

Evelyn rose from the bed, feeling so plain next to Annie. Her friend was decked out in the latest fashion she'd whipped up for herself.

Evelyn nearly stopped at the sight before her. She'd never seen Jesse in a suit before. His white shirt didn't have a speck of dirt; she'd never seen his clothes without some dust on them. Even his coat looked new, and the fancy dress shoes beneath his dress pants were shined to perfection.

Suddenly she wished more than anything that she had spent more time fixing herself up in front of the vanity mirror.

She felt a hand link with hers. "You look beautiful, Evelyn." John gave her an appreciative look up and down. She felt more violated than flattered.

"You look lovely, Annie." Evelyn turned her head at Jesse's compliment to her best friend. Her jaw clenched. Why should she care what he thought of Annie?

Annie fanned herself with her hand and began batting her lashes as if she was competing with someone for most blinks in a second. "Why, thank you, Jesse Greenwood. You look dashing as well, if I dare say so myself."

Oh, she dared all right. Evelyn felt the back of her eyes sting as she watched him offer his arm to Annie and lead them outside to his buggy. He held out his hand as a balance before she climbed inside, and she placed her palm in his to take a seat. She noticed the smug smile on Annie's face as she sat inside the buggy.

"Evelyn, is something the matter?" John's forehead creased as he studied her expression, all the while tugging her forward, out the door and to his own horse and buggy.

She managed a weak smile. "Oh, nothing. Just thinking of the wedding, that is all." She followed John outside, her arm still wrapped around his. When had Jesse ever offered his hand to her? She'd always been the one reaching for his hand, making an effort to close the distance between them. All Annie had to do was bat her eyes and suddenly he was slipping his arm around her?

The ride to the church was the longest of Evelyn's life. The entire time, she watched Annie lean her head against Jesse's shoulder, her arm tucked around his. Evelyn had never seen her so suddenly enamored with a man. None of her previous infatuations had been this strong.

Jesse did nothing to push her off. Her head just rested there, nestled in the crevice between his shoulder and neck. The two looked like a classic couple from a novel, the beautiful romantic redhead and the rough cowboy. A novel that Evelyn had no place in.

She pursed her lips. "Annie's and Jesse's behavior is hardly proper. They are not even formally courting."

John ignored her comment, his hands gripped on the reins. She had dropped her arm from his at this point.

"Out in the open like that," she continued. She lifted her chin. "They should be ashamed of themselves, really. If Annie's mother could see her—"

"Why do you care about Annie and Jesse?" John turned to Evelyn again. He tried to pat her hand, but she instead drew her arms tighter against herself. He sighed. "I do not know what is making you upset today. We should enjoy the wedding, should we not? We will be the groom and bride soon enough."

Evelyn felt fear stir inside her. He hinted too much at marriage. No, they weren't even hints. He basically declared their marriage as an inevitable occurrence when he hadn't even properly asked. She swallowed hard. "We should talk about something else."

"All right." John began another tirade about the history of Hamilton's roads, and she felt herself lose interest once again. He wouldn't ask her opinion anyway. John was an honest and respectable man, she firmly believed so. But he wasn't very interested in what she had to say.

She wasn't particularly interested in his words either. No, the scene before her was much more engrossing. Her gaze drifted back to Jesse and Annie. She tried not to think about how much his arm around Annie's bothered her.

She especially tried not to think about Jesse's arm being around hers instead.

•••

Jesse helped Annie out of the buggy. One of her legs dangled as she stepped out of the carriage, hesitating over whether or not to step down. To his surprise, she skipped over one of the steps and fell forward. He caught her at the last moment with both arms.

She smiled up at him, but he furrowed his brow. Why had she tripped on purpose? "Be careful."

"You seem awfully concerned for my safety, Mr. Greenwood." Annie threw her curls back, the long, red waves falling over one of her shoulders. She did the fast blinking thing again. Maybe she did have something in her eye.

Before he could reply, John Cooper's voice boomed out from the next buggy. "Good catch, Mr. Greenwood!"

He looked over at John and immediately wished he hadn't. John kissed Evelyn's hand as she stepped out. Her cheeks flushed the prettiest of pink shades as John slipped his arm in hers. Whatever she said about his character, Jesse couldn't help comparing his treatment of her to a farmer possessive of an expensive animal. He treated her like his property more than his sweetheart.

"Mr. Greenwood seems not only useful at catching cattle—he's skilled at catching women as well." John grinned from ear to ear, as if he'd just told some great joke. Annie immediately started squealing with laughter.

Jesse came up with a million insulting replies as he ignored John and turned in the direction of the church.

The area in front of the building was filled with a heap of people. He hadn't realized Loretta invited so many. Billowing dresses and tailored coats filled every nook and cranny. He recognized a handful of people, some from the ranch and some of Loretta's friends. But the rest of the faces were a mystery to him. It looked like she'd invited all of Hamilton and Harleigh.

During the ceremony, he and Annie found their seats in the pew directly behind Evelyn and John. Evelyn had piled her dark hair into a high bun at the top of her head. She wore a blue dress, nearly black in the darkness of the church, but a vibrant navy blue in the light.

Jesse tried to keep his eyes off the back of her neck during the entire ceremony and focus on Loretta, but his eyes were unable to remain on the groom and bride for long. What was she thinking? Was she considering marriage with John? But the sight of her soft black curls wouldn't tell him what she was planning. He wished more than anything to know her thoughts.

When the ceremony finished, he finally pulled his eyes away from her long enough to study Loretta and Preston. They'd spruced themselves up, that was certain. Loretta had pulled her hair into an elegant loose bun at the nape of her neck, and even Preston looked sharp in his wedding suit.

But not everything was different. Jesse had never seen a gaze filled with more love than the way Preston gazed at Loretta. He frowned—he'd nearly split them apart. His sister didn't deserve a man from a higher social standing; she deserved the man who had captured her heart.

The bride and groom were the first to walk down the aisle. The crowd stood up from the pews and started forward, all desperate to catch the bride's colorful bouquet. Loretta laughed and threw the collection of bright flowers high into the air. She'd thrown it far, nearly back toward the altar. Jesse watched the flowers fly over his own head and behind him into—

His heart lurched.

Evelyn held up the bouquet high in the air, a wide smile on her face. She waved it in the air, and several groans were heard from both sides of the pews. Others around her congratulated her, and even Annie leaned over to whisper something in her ear. Whatever Annie said, it made her laugh. She was positively radiant as she held the flowers in her hands.

Then John gripped her arm tightly against him. Evelyn squirmed away at first, then stood still as he maintained the steel hold. Her shoulders drooped, and the bouquet hung at her side without the enthusiasm she'd possessed only moments ago.

Jesse set his jaw. John didn't love her. Not like he did, anyway. Why couldn't she see that?

Avoiding John and Evelyn proved to be easy enough after the wedding. The entire crowd that had squeezed into the church was more than grateful to be back in the open air. Couples of all ages danced in the center of a ring that had formed in the clearing. The saloon, alarmingly close to the church, served to make his fellow ranch hands louder and rowdier than normal. Young children played a game under the supervision of some of their parents. Everywhere he looked, there was a group of people laughing and talking, still high off the happiness of the wedding.

Annie found no shortage of folks to introduce him to. Every conversation she dragged him into was the same. After introducing him first, she would gush to her friends how handsome he was, as if he weren't standing right next to her.

He was glad when she pulled him away from the girls. She picked up two sarsaparillas from a nearby counter and handed one to him. He wouldn't have minded some whiskey right then, but he popped the top off the sarsaparilla anyway and took a long sip.

"So…" Annie's finger twirled around one of the loose strawberry curls that fell from her bun. "How's your stay in Hamilton been so far, Mr. Greenwood?"

"Call me Jesse." He tried to focus his eyes on her, but just like during the ceremony, he found his eyes scanning the crowd for a glimpse of dark hair and a blue dress. "Hamilton's the same as I remember."

"I can't imagine ever leaving this place. Can you ever imagine living in a town more wonderful?" She gestured to the crowd with the hand that wasn't holding her sarsaparilla. "It's home to me."

"It is to me, too." He looked down at his opened bottle, and then set it down on the counter. "I've considered staying in Hamilton before."

"Oh, you don't still want to leave for California, do you? I know it must be exciting and all, but nothing quite compares to home." Annie brought both hands to each side of her cheeks in an exaggerated movement. Her sarsaparilla bottle nearly fell out of her hand. He grabbed it from her before it could shatter on the ground.

"So considerate." She pointed to the trail leading away from the church. Her voice was perky, like nothing could bring down her spirits. "Say, I was hoping to talk to you alone. Do you want to go for a walk with me and get away from here for a while?"

He shook his head. "Think I'll just stay here for now." He pointed at Loretta and Preston, who'd joined the group of dancing couples. "Can't believe I ever wanted to split 'em up."

Skirts of every color and cloth, full and twirling, flew out as the men picked up their partners and set them back down. Green dresses, red dresses, blue dresses—Jesse's eyes focused on the image of the woman in the navy blue dress.

He pushed away from leaning against the counter and straightened his coat. "Excuse me, Annie." He walked away from her and toward the throng of couples in the center. The entire time his eyes remained fixed on Evelyn.

The song had just ended, and the band was deciding the next song to play while the couples stood patiently in the center. He strode up to the beautiful woman in the blue dress and tapped her on the shoulder. The man next to her scowled, but Jesse didn't care.

He extended his hand. "How about the next dance?"

Her eyes widened. She didn't protest, though. Jesse could feel John's scrutinizing glare at the back of his neck as John walked away.

Jesse placed one hand on the small of her back, and the other was outstretched to hold hers. The music started again, and they spun and stepped to the beat. The music was slower than the previous song, and the couples danced in an easy manner, chatting among themselves.

Evelyn peered over his shoulder, probably to check if John was out of earshot. She must have been satisfied because she said to Jesse, "What are you trying to do?"

"Dance with one of my friends." He smirked as he noticed her cheeks flush. His chest was pressed close to hers, and he could almost hear her heart beating. "Reckon there's no harm in that."

"One song only."

"Why's that?"

"You just pushed John away. He traveled here with me, not you."

"I know. I have to tell you something, though."

She sighed. "Tell me what? You'd better have a reason—"

"I see the way he looks at you. It's like you're his possession, not someone he cherishes. How well does he even know you?"

He felt Evelyn's body stiffen against his. "What do you mean?"

Jesse's mind raced. There was only so long until the dance ended and she'd be back in John's arms again. He needed to say something to get her away from this man. Anything. He couldn't stand seeing her being so close to Cooper a second longer.

"Come with me."

"Are you out of mind?"

"Just do it."

"Come with you where?"

Maybe he was a little out of his mind. He didn't know where. All he knew was that he couldn't stand the way he saw John looking at her out of the corner of his eye. He needed to take her someplace where John couldn't find them. A place all to their own.

A memory flashed before his eyes. *Of course.* He tugged at her hand, but she resisted. They stopped dancing in the center of the circle. Couples danced around them, a colorful blend of skirts and suits.

"It's just for a little while. We'll come back if you want to."

"Jesse, I doubt I can just leave John here—"

"Trust me."

She fixed him a wary eye, but she allowed him to guide her away. By the time John realized what was happening and caught up to them, she was sitting in Jesse's buggy.

"Evelyn, come down from there this minute."

Jesse tipped his hat to John. "Take Annie back to her home when she wants to leave. Evelyn and I need to sort out something on the ranch for a while, Mr. Cooper."

With a flap of his reins, the horses started forward and away from a fuming John Cooper. The roll of the wooden buggy wheels tuned out John's sounds of protest from behind them. They left the wedding guests behind as the horses headed back up the trail.

Eventually Evelyn recognized the road.

"Why are we going back to Breighton?" She raised an eyebrow. "All the ranch hands are still down there in Harleigh. They have finished the work for today."

"Do you still go out into the pastures?" He turned to her and smiled. "How far do you still venture out there?"

"Not any farther than the barbed wire," she said slowly. She brushed a lock of hair behind her ear and shook her head. "I hope you are actually taking me somewhere, Jesse. There is no reason to come back to Breighton so early."

"You'll see." He continued the buggy further down the trail, past Evelyn's house. Where the big house ended, another road began. The cleared path followed a neighboring ranch's corral, the sturdy wooden posts marking the way to their destination.

He finally stopped, and heard her draw in a quick intake of breath.

The white gazebo stood ahead of them, the same as he had remembered it from all those years ago. The paint had faded, and he reckoned a fine layer of dust had settled on the floor. Otherwise, the gazebo was exactly the same as it had been on the last day he'd seen Evelyn before she left for the East Coast. The exact same as all the days they'd spent hiding away from her father. The exact same as the time they'd been in love with one another.

He helped her out of the buggy. They walked to the gazebo together, down the road lined with pebbles. While the nostalgia was overwhelming, so was the foreign sense of intrusion. He hadn't walked this road in years.

By the looks of it, she hadn't either. Her slender hands traced the white posts, her fingertips skimming over the chipped paint like she'd never seen a gazebo before. "I haven't been here since..." She didn't need to finish her sentence.

"Me too."

She stepped out beyond the gazebo and sat down on the pasture. Jesse settled beside her, both of them looking out onto the neighboring ranch.

"It was here, wasn't it?" Evelyn threaded her fingers through the long grass, as if her touch could mark the spot. "We were here, seven years ago, making that promise. What were the words again?" She let out a bitter laugh. "*No one can ever stop us from…* oh, what was it? No one can stop us from…"

"No one can stop us from loving one another." The quote had never left his memory. "Then I promised to never stop writing to you."

"I promised to never give you up." Evelyn brought her knees forward, her skirt draping over her legs. She smoothed out the cloth over her shins. "It seems funny, does it not? When we were young, there was no such thing as a broken promise. I could not even imagine why it would ever happen."

"We couldn't predict the future."

"Of course not. We were so young. There's no way to anticipate life and all the challenges it brings."

"The promises don't have to be broken." His voice was low. He leaned forward, closing the distance between them. The wind blew against Evelyn's forehead, sending the few tendrils framing her face dancing in the wind. He brushed a lock of stray hair behind her ear.

She winced. "You cannot do that."

"Do what?"

"Look at me like that." Evelyn nibbled her lower lip. His attention turned to her mouth. He cradled one hand behind her head, and her breathing started to come in quick intakes. "Touch me like that."

"Like this?" He pressed his lips against hers for what felt like the first time. She tasted like strawberries and honeysuckle and peppermints. He leaned forward, pinning her against the grass. Half of his mind expected her to push him off, to run away and back to John.

But Evelyn crushed her own lips against his with equal passion. She arched her body against him, removing whatever little distance remained. Her hands roamed through his hair. She opened her mouth and pressed her tongue against his lips, and gave everything she had into the kiss when he opened his mouth.

She rolled him over until he was pinned underneath her. When they drew away to finally gasp for breath, she'd already started to unbutton the length of his clean white shirt, or formerly clean at least. He had never cared that much about the shirt anyway. She chucked it next to them and leaned back against his body, undulating her narrow hips against his.

He'd finally had a taste of Evelyn Lancaster, and now he couldn't get enough of his fill.

His pants became uncomfortably tight when she moaned against his kiss. He brought his mouth down away from her mouth, along her jawline, and down her collarbone. His lips grazed the crevice between her breasts, and she moaned again.

Her hands roamed across his bare chest, tracing an outline of abdominal muscles. Every place she touched sent a shock through his chest. Her small fingers caressed the muscles of his arms, running up and down his biceps. Evelyn continued to arch against him. Her soft body above his own hard muscle drove him mad.

She gasped as he massaged her breasts through the fabric of her dress, which only encouraged him to continue his ministrations.

"You drive me crazy," he murmured against the nape of her neck. He wished they could stay like this forever.

"You drive me crazy, too..." She moaned, pressing her body against him. She felt so incredibly wonderful against him. "This is crazy..."

Her body stiffened. Suddenly, she pulled away from Jesse. It was more like she literally pushed him away, sending his body falling back to the ground with a hard *thud*. Her head was shaking, and she began to back away.

"This is crazy," she repeated. "What am I doing?"

"What do you mean?"

"I am courted by *John Cooper*. Not you." She squeezed her eyes shut tight, then flashed them open. An emotion he could only describe as confusion was written all across her face. "I need to leave."

"Evelyn, wait!" He picked up his shirt and started after her, but she spun around and pointed a finger at him.

"Do not dare come any closer to me." She shook her index finger at him, as if scolding a child. "The gazebo is not far from Breighton. I can walk."

He pulled his arms back into the sleeves of the shirt. "That's ridiculous. I have the horses and buggy here."

"I am fine, I assure you."

Jesse buttoned his shirt. "Reckon it'd be faster if you just rode me."

Her eyes widened.

"With me. Rode *with* me." He cursed under his breath. "I meant ride with me."

She shook her head. "I said I'll *walk*." Evelyn's voice was hard. Her arms were folded across her chest, as if denying him all visual access to her body as well. "Just go. I need some time alone to think."

"Evelyn—"

"I said go!"

There was no use in trying to argue with her. With a heavy heart, he sat back up on the buggy and started back to Breighton.

He looked over his shoulder. Evelyn hadn't started walking yet. She just stood there, standing in the middle of the gazebo, staring out at the rolling green pastures stretched before her. She'd always looked regal, with her chin held slightly up and a determined look in her eye.

His fingers itched to stop the horses and turn back the buggy. He wanted to jump out and kiss her again, press her lithe body against the grass of the pasture until her lips agreed to stay with him.

He groaned, running one hand through his hair while the other gripped the reins. Not that she would, if her "time to think" response was anything to go by. She was always trying to make sense of a situation. He had no doubt her mind was racing with the consequences of their kiss.

He would have given anything to know what she was thinking.

# CHAPTER ELEVEN

The door to Loretta's house was propped wide open. Evelyn found that odd, considering Loretta told her that she and Preston decided to stay in Harleigh for another week before coming back to Hamilton. Had Loretta decided to stay here after all?

"Loretta? I just finished unpacking the last of your..." The voice at the top of the stairs trailed off. He walked down the steps one heavy *thud* of his boots at a time, his eyes studying the figure in the doorway.

"Hello, Jesse." She gulped. Images of their indiscretion the day before flooded her senses and threatened all common sense. Traitorous body. No, she wouldn't let that happen again.

"Hello there, Eve."

She pointed over her shoulder. "I saw Loretta's door open, and I thought maybe your sister had returned early. You seem very busy, though. I think I will just be leaving now."

"Stay."

She turned her head at the sound of his voice. His face was an expressionless mask, but there was urgency in his tone.

"I'm in no hurry. I just finished unpacking the last of the items Loretta told me to." He reached the end of the steps and gestured to the parlor. "Stay for a while."

Against her better judgment, Evelyn walked into the parlor.

"I have something to tell you." His words came out slowly, almost hesitant. "Something I've been wanting to tell you for a while."

Yes, definitely against her better judgment. She knew her cheeks were blushing that embarrassing shade of pink again as panic set in. "John Cooper has expressed interest in me." He was the one who'd remained steadfast and cared for her. He'd written the letters, not Jesse.

"You wouldn't want to be with him anymore if I told you the truth."

"What truth?"

"The truth is that I care for you, Eve Lancaster."

"Care for me? Since when? You and Annie looked cozy at Loretta's wedding." She spied his confused gaze and scoffed. *The nerve.* "Do not tell me you used her. You used my best friend to make me jealous?"

"Annie? I don't care for Annie any more than a friend."

"And that is how I thought you saw me." Evelyn placed her hands on her hips. "That is why I agreed to allow John to court me."

"I don't think you're listening to me. I care for you."

"And? How long would it have taken to tell me this," she snapped back, "if I had not struck up a relationship with John? When would you have finally told me you cared?"

She watched his jaw clench. "I wasn't willing to take the risk again—"

"But I was!" Her fists itched to punch against his solid chest. She wanted nothing more than to take out all her frustration and anger at their situation on him. "I was willing to begin a relationship with you again."

"How was I to know?"

Her jaw dropped. "I tried! I held your hand, I told you I missed you, I gave you signs!"

"You gave me nothing."

"As if it matters anymore! It is too late. You have already given Annie such false hope and I have… John just inspired jealousy within you." Her heart ached even as she reasoned out Jesse's territorial behavior. It was common among old flames, a sudden spark of envy over what was once his. It didn't mean anything. "You were not going to admit you cared for me otherwise."

"I rescued you from a burning barn!" He paced back and forth in front of her, then stopped. "What else could you want?"

"I want communication. I want you to finally tell me how you feel about me without having to do so because another man takes interest." She bit her bottom lip. "I am forever grateful that you saved my life in that barn. But that action alone could not have allowed me to assume you loved me."

"I do. I love you, Evelyn Lancaster."

"Why now?" She swallowed hard. If only he'd told her earlier.

"You're the one I've always cared for, Eve. But if Cooper's the one you want, then go. Go back to him. He doesn't love you, you know. He's a powerful rich fella, and you're a powerful rich girl."

"Since when has his being rich become a negative?"

"He only cares about you for your ranch and social standing. You can see it in the way he treats you."

Evelyn felt her blood boil as anger clouded her vision in an instant. A strangled sound of frustration escaped her throat. "How dare you! Can a man only love me because of my social standing? He sincerely cares for me, Jesse. I know he does."

"No one else loves you like I do."

"You pulled away from me every time I tried to talk to you!" She wiped away the tears threatening to fall from the corners of her eyes. A dull ache throbbed in her chest, the tempo matching the hurt beating in her heart. "How was I supposed to have any idea how you felt about me?"

"You think I didn't want to?" He seethed. Evelyn drew back. She'd never seen him so impassioned before. "What was I supposed to do while you were entertaining John—kick up a row? I was terrified, Eve. I was scared to death of *this* happening."

"What? What is this?"

"Putting my heart on my sleeve, telling you how I feel." He shook his head. "What's the point? You already chose that John fella anyway."

"Now don't go pinning this on me! You were so offish all the time. You never told me you cared for me." Her fists clenched around her dress, wrinkling the cotton pleats.

"I did! I told you, didn't I?" Jesse ran a hand through his hair, yanking slightly on the ends as he finished each sentence. "I said I missed when you were mine."

She scoffed. "Missing me isn't enough. You never asked to court me. You never admitted you felt anything for me. I was not even sure if you considered us *friends*."

"No, Eve." His voice was low, and the rumble of his tone made her knees quiver. "We can never be just friends. For us, it's all or nothing."

She took a step back. "What about Annie?"

He furrowed his brow. "What about her?"

"She thinks she's going to *marry* you, and you do not even care about her feelings."

Jesse narrowed his eyes. "Hold on a minute. I said nothing to her about marriage. I took her to this wedding, and that was all."

Evelyn had to admit to herself Annie was prone to delusions. Annie always assumed too much from her relationships with men. But how could she be the reason her friend experienced another heartbreak?

He placed his calloused hands on her arms. His touch made her body want to sink into his embrace, to clasp her arms around his neck as he held her waist. "Evelyn, I have enough money saved up from California. I can support you. You don't have to marry anyone else."

She steeled her shoulders. "You told me to think about if I could go back in time to that day when you left for California."

"I remember."

"You asked me if I would have run away with you. You asked me if I would give up my family, my friends, my ranch, everything I knew for you. I could not answer then, but I know what my answer would be now."

Jesse remained as still as a statue. She swore if she dropped a needle, the sound would echo off the walls of the parlor.

"My answer would be no."

His shoulders slumped.

She continued, unfazed by his reaction. "Annie told me love creates a home. She is right. I love my family, I love my friends, I love taking care of Breighton and watching the ranch prosper. I have traveled to the East Coast and will not go another day without seeing a Texas sunset. If you really loved me, you would not ask me to leave my home for you."

"I never did ask," he muttered.

"Because you already knew what my answer would be." She pressed her lips together. Evelyn could feel him slipping away from her, like a thread that was slowly stretching taut. "You already knew I would not follow you. I used to think I would. I thought I would have followed you anywhere, done anything as long as it was with you."

"You could still pursue a career if you came with me. You could leave Breighton."

A lump formed at the back of throat. "I wanted that life once. But I want to help run Breighton now. That's my future."

"Is there a place for me in that future?"

Evelyn blinked back the tear that was threatening to fall down her cheek. "No. My place is here, whether or not you decide to stay."

Jesse remained silent. He walked over to the window, as if he'd spotted something odd. The translucent curtain was drawn back. When he finally spoke, his voice was gruff. "You've made your choice, it seems. He's here."

He walked out of the doorway just as John Cooper stepped in. She held her breath as he brushed past John without so much as a glance.

The moment Jesse left the room, she finally let her tears fall. John was bent over with her in a moment. She felt his arms wrap around her chest. He shushed her, wiping away her tears with the backs of his hands. "What's wrong, darlin'? I saw your horse hitched up in front of Loretta's house and thought there might be trouble."

Her eyes narrowed. "Trouble? What trouble?"

"Jesse Greenwood. That man is nothing but quick on the draw. The cowboy just made you cry, didn't he?"

"Oh, he would not look for such trouble." Evelyn pulled away. This was ridiculous. Was her choice really John? The more time she spent with him, the more time she spent avoiding him. He hadn't even responded to her letter.

John watched her as if afraid she would burst into hysterics at any moment. "Sure doesn't look like nothing."

"Why did you never respond to my letter?"

He blinked. "Letter? What letter?"

"The one I left for you in the knothole." She said her words with a deliberate slowness. An uneasy feeling settled over her while she studied his shocked expression with a wary eye. "I was replying to the one you left for me."

"Why would I leave you a letter in a tree?" John laughed.

"You said you wrote them."

The laughter stopped. "Don't shoot your mouth off, Evelyn. I can see you whenever I want."

"No." Her voice was hard. "It's not nonsense. The day I gave you permission to court me, I saw you reading my letter. That letter was a reply to the ones I was receiving. You said you were the man writing them to me."

He continued to stare blankly for several moments, and then his eyes lit up in understanding. "Oh, that was so long ago, I forgot about that." He sputtered, looking around the room as if the walls would provide him with the right words to say. "How am I supposed to remember a few measly letters? I could have written them if you'd asked me to."

She couldn't believe her ears. All this time, she'd been justifying her alliance with John based on his respectable, honest disposition. "Answer my question: Did you write the letters?"

He made a halting motion with his hand, as if it would stop her from figuring him out. "Now before you start accusing me of lying—"

Wind whooshed past Evelyn's ears.

He wasn't honest at all. She'd fallen for all his soft solder. "You did not write those letters, did you?"

"Let's not start a little fuss." He held out both his hands now, as if trying to calm a bucking horse. "Lying about the letters was just my way of showing I care about you. What does it matter if I wrote you or not?"

Foolishness washed over Evelyn in choppy waves. She suddenly felt like hand-blown glass, completely transparent and completely breakable. How could she have been so blind?

"I was beginning my courtship with you through those letters."

"Oh, that is rich! I do not wish to *begin* anything with you anymore. You lied to me."

"So? What's a little lie here and there compared to a lifetime of marriage?" He reached out and grasped her hand. She recoiled from his touch as if he were a rattler. "With my parents' money, and your father's land, we'll be the richest couple in all of Hamilton."

Her heart sank. *Wrong*, that's what she'd been. She'd been all wrong about him.

"Besides wealth, what else do you love about me?"

He let out a low laugh, as if she was being ridiculous. "Don't catch me off guard like that, dearest Evelyn. You love my wealth as well."

She hadn't really known John at all. And he certainly didn't know her.

"Social class and riches do not concern me. I care about my ranch, and I do not want to marry anyone who is only looking to exploit it through the alliance."

John huffed, as if she'd deeply offended him. "Exploit? We would merely be using your land as another source of income. No one said anything about exploiting."

"Is this why you wanted to marry me all this time?"

"Why do you think I waited so long?" John placed his hands on his hips like a petulant child. Even through his annoyance, he still looked handsome in that classic way, the kind girls immortalized in dime novels about selfless and handsome heroes. To think she'd once believed he had the personality of one as well. "We are the most suited for each other in this town. Everyone else is beneath us."

She'd been so blind. "Beneath us? You wanted to court me because you believed the other girls were socially inferior?"

He stiffened. "It's about what's proper. Don't you care about marrying within your social class?"

"I do not care a continental about class." Her lip curled in disgust. "Was everything else a lie as well? You said you cared for me."

"And I do." John looked at her as if she was a fool. "A marriage is a merger. People like us don't marry for love, or care for people because we want to. We marry who's respectable. We love who's respectable."

"Would you still want to be with me if my family didn't own Breighton?"

John huffed in indignation.

Evelyn shook her head. "I never want to see you again, John Cooper. You are never welcome to Breighton."

He dusted off his coat and sneered at her. "You'll regret this, Evelyn. You should have been *honored* I was still interested in you. No one else in this town will have you."

She watched him unhitch his horse and ride away from the house as quickly as he could. The image of his retreating form brought nothing but a sigh of relief when he was finally gone.

Regret turning him down? Somehow, she didn't think she would.

But she did feel played out after that exchange. At least she didn't have to worry about that mudsill again.

She waited in Loretta's house by the window for a few more hours, hoping Jesse would return. Surely once he'd cooled down he'd return to Loretta's house. She didn't know why she waited for him, exactly. After the last heated exchange, there wasn't much else to say.

But she couldn't suppress the overwhelming urge in her chest to see him again.

•••

Dearest love,

I reckon it's time I stepped out of the shadows and revealed who's been writing these letters to you. Judging from your choice of John Cooper, you've probably seen these letters as just an amusement to pass the time. But if you have found any joy in reading my words, then writing these letters has been time well spent.

I never did break my promise to keep writing to you. Yesterday in the gazebo was one of the best days I've had in a long time. I'd face any outlaw in a duel if only to kiss you. I thought I'd never taste your sweet lips again. Half of my mind knew you'd respond; the other half knew you'd step back. But if you're going to spend a lifetime with another man, the least I wanted was a small kiss before I never saw you again.

I started these letters as a way to express myself to you. You keep saying I never said anything, I never told you… I did, Eve. I just didn't have the courage to say it under my name. Every compliment, every sweet remark, every word of these letters still rings true.

I'm not much for talking. Seeing you in person always seems to keep me tongue-tied and unable to say what I want. These letters were my way to speak to you. You've always been wonderful with words, but so is John. He's the smooth talker you want. Not me.

You're right. I didn't ask you to leave with me for California because I knew you wouldn't go. That's one of the parts of your personality I love the most, Eve. You're strong. You have been dedicated to managing the ranch. You have a spark inside you, a fire that makes decisions with confidence and sticks with them till the end.

But I didn't start this letter to start jawing with praise. This is my last letter to you, Eve. I'm writing this letter to say goodbye. I've overstayed my welcome in Hamilton under your roof. It gets harder and harder every day to see John place his arm around yours. Pretty soon you'll marry him. Call me weak if you want, but I can't stand to see you in his arms in your wedding gown.

I can't even stay here long enough to see you look at him the way you once looked at me.

You keep referencing the past between us, bringing up all the memories I once tried to forget. I attempt to shrug them off most of the time, pretend like I don't know what you're talking about. I lied, Eve. I never forgot. When I left for California, the only thought that kept me going forward was the incentive that I'd get rich for you, that I'd come back for you. I did become rich, but then I became scared.

I was terrified of returning for you and then leaving without you, as I do now. Every day I worked in California, I repeated a different memory I had of you in my mind. I imagined that night in the gazebo, when you taught me how to dance. I remembered that time in the corral, when I taught you how to saddle a horse. I thought of those late nights out on the pastures when I was just fifteen, and we taught each other how to love.

You taught me how to trust someone.

Can't blame me for leaving when you shattered the trust between us. I blamed you then, but I won't now. You've moved on with your life, and I can't hold you back.

Sorry about the lying, by the way. I know you keep jawing about how honest and decent John is. I'm happy you've found a man who would never lie to you.

Yet I can't imagine you finding a man who loves you more than I do.

Jesse

He signed the letter and sealed it in an envelope. Jesse stood up from the oak rocker and placed the envelope between the two posts. After reaching into his pocket, he pulled out the honeysuckle he'd plucked on the way back to the ranch. He wondered if she'd even bother to look at the letter, now that she'd chosen John. She might just burn it.

He jumped from the porch down to the dirt ground, landing with a plume of dust covering his boots. Had he packed everything? He walked over to the wagon, checking to make sure all his items were secured. It was nearly time to go now. He lifted a few more boxes from the ground and into the wagon.

He stood back, trying to think of anything he'd neglected to bring for the journey back to California. The horses were bridled, and the saddle was in place.

"Forget anything?"

Jesse turned around to face Mr. Lancaster. The boss's arms were folded over his chest, and he leaned his long frame against one of the white porch posts instead of his usual cane.

"Glad to see your illness has passed, sir."

"You're forgettin' to say your goodbyes, Mr. Greenwood."

Jesse approached Mr. Lancaster. The porch floorboards creaked underneath his weight as he stood before him. "You don't need me around the ranch anymore."

Mr. Lancaster placed both of his hands on Jesse's shoulders. "I used to want you out of this house more than anything."

Jesse squared his shoulders. "Sir…"

"And now, I would do anything within my power to make you stay."

He rubbed the back of his neck. "Reckon I'm more of a nuisance than a help here to some people."

Mr. Lancaster clucked his tongue. "You know as well as I that the only person you're referring to is Evelyn." He shook his head. "She doesn't see you as a nuisance, Jesse. Far from it. The girl's balled up, that's all. Twenty-three and she still can't make up her mind."

"Make up her mind about what, sir?"

Mr. Lancaster gave a sly smile. "About whether to admit now she's loved you all her life, or admit it to you later."

He nearly stepped backward in surprise. Jesse thought back to her refusal of him—two refusals in two days, actually. He reckoned it was better her father didn't find out about the kiss, though. "I talked to her today, and she said her place was here. She has no interest in going out further west."

"Your place is here, too." Mr. Lancaster nodded, a mixture of newfound respect and friendliness in his eyes. Jesse could still remember when those eyes had flashed a warning. Time changed all of them. "You know it as well as I. You saved this ranch when you had every reason not to."

"Anyone would have."

"Not just anyone. You're a man I can tie to. I'm proud to know you."

"I'm just used to being a granger, that's all. I've wound up my business here, Mr. Lancaster. I should be heading out."

"No matter what those folks in California may offer you, your home is here at Breighton."

Well, it wouldn't be his home anymore if John Cooper moved in. The thought of Eve and her flannel-mouthed future fiancé made him scowl.

"If this is about that Mr. Cooper, I doubt her courtship with him will last long," Mr. Lancaster said.

Jesse couldn't suppress the curiosity in his tone. "Why not?"

"Because she loves you. She always has. She always will." Mr. Lancaster chuckled. "I remember when I was like you, wanting to separate my daughter and you the same way you wanted to separate Preston and Loretta. You can scold them all you want till you're blue in the face, but love won't listen to anybody."

His throat was dry. "I told her I loved her, sir. She didn't seem to feel the same."

Mr. Lancaster pressed his mouth into a firm line. He held his palm out, and Jesse shook his hand with a firm grip. "Which way you headed?"

"Stopping at Raleigh for the night. Then I'll head on over the border."

"That's a mighty long ride you got there before sunset." He tipped his hat at Jesse. "I wish you well, Jesse Greenwood. Breighton is always open to you."

Jesse nodded and headed back onto the driver's seat of the wagon. He'd barely just gripped the reins when Mr. Lancaster called out, "Don't you want to wait to say goodbye to Evelyn?"

As if she'd even want to see him again. He glanced over at the tree where he'd placed the envelope. The bright honeysuckle covered the edges of the letter, but her name could still be clearly seen through the petals.

One last letter.

"I've already said goodbye to her, sir."

•••

Evelyn slowed her horse to a halt in front of Annie Inglewood.

"Annie?"

It sure looked like Annie, but at the same time this girl was acting nothing like her. Annie's shoulders were slumped, and she sat on the bench in front of the general store with a resignation Evelyn had never seen in her friend before.

Annie looked up at the sound of her name and perked up her shoulders when she saw Evelyn. She smoothed out the front of her dress.

Evelyn stepped down out of the stirrups and off of the saddle, frowning. "Why do you look so upset?"

"He doesn't care for me." Annie shook her head. Her voice sounded thick, like she was stifling tears. "Jesse doesn't care for me after all. It was all a delusion. So much for being sweethearts."

Evelyn pursed her lips. As much as she wanted to remind Annie that she'd just seen him a few days ago and had spent only a few hours with him, her friend's defeated expression stopped her.

Instead, she sat down next to Annie and put her arm around Annie's shoulder. Annie leaned in, sniffling into her dress.

"I think I know why he doesn't care for me."

"Maybe he does not want to court anyone. It has nothing to do with you."

"No, I know who he really wants."

Evelyn's stomach tightened. She continued to rub Annie's shoulders. Maybe if she stayed silent, Annie would change the topic.

No such luck.

"He was talking to me, you know, and I was so sure that he was going to ask to court me. And then… then he just walked right on over to you. As if he couldn't care less about me."

"Oh, I am sure that is not true. He does care about you."

She let out a bitter laugh. "You don't have to lie to me. He doesn't care for me the way I care about him."

"Maybe he does. Just give him time." Her own heart ached as she said the words.

"He doesn't want me. He never will. Not as a sweetheart. Not the same way I love him." Annie paused her sniffling to look up at Evelyn. "Not the same way he wants you."

"I know."

Annie's forehead creased as she blinked at her friend in confusion. "You do?"

Evelyn swallowed. "He told me so a few hours ago." She stared down at her clasped hands, eyes downcast. Her lower lip trembled. The words kept tumbling out before she could contain them. "I know you care for him. Annie, I swear I did not intend to hurt you in any way."

Annie shushed her. "It's not your fault. It's not anyone's fault." The moisture at the ends of her eyes had dried up. "I am shocked, though."

Evelyn frowned. "About?"

"Why do you seem so upset about it?" Annie tilted her head to the side, considering the matter. "Oh, surely you told him that you felt the same way, didn't you?"

She bit her lower lip. "I did not tell him anything, really. I was so afraid of betraying you, or betraying John… one of you would have been so hurt."

"So you hurt Jesse instead."

Evelyn's gaze drifted down to her hands, clasped in her lap. "I… I thought he was too late to admit his feelings for me."

"It's never too late. What would you have told him?" Annie leaned closer to her friend. "He practically left you a California widow. What would you have said to him, if you weren't worrying about what other people thought?"

"I'd tell him I loved him." The confessions left her lips before she could stop herself and consider her words. She spoke with a hesitant manner, as if her words stumped her. "I think I always have. I never stopped loving him."

Annie sighed. "I feared as much. You two have been inseparable since you were thirteen. He has a case of you, Evelyn. There's no room in his heart for another girl."

"But you should know I told him that it was wrong for him to flirt with you and lead you on without a second thought."

Annie waved her hand in dismissal. "Oh, there was never any flirting. I could tell he wasn't truly paying attention to a word I was saying at the wedding." Her friend managed a small, sad smile. "I'm not blind. His eyes stayed fixed on you the entire time."

Her heart hammered within her chest. She hadn't been able to glance at him during the ceremony. The idea of him staring at her during the wedding both thrilled and terrified her.

"Especially when you caught that bouquet," Annie continued. "I would give anything for a man to look at me the same way he looked at you in that moment."

Evelyn remembered the way Jesse had gazed at her outside the gazebo before they kissed. It was as if she was made of hand-blown glass, and with one wrong move she would slip from his fingers and shatter. Their relationship wasn't shattered glass, though, she mused.

Why hadn't she recognized Jesse's feelings earlier? John and his letters had been her major concern. But John had lied to her, and whoever had written the letters wasn't coming forward.

Clarity filled the crevices of her mind. A situation that had once seemed so difficult started to simplify, breaking down the worries that had prevented her from opening her heart. She did love Jesse. She'd never admitted the fact to herself before. Fear of untold consequences and possible misunderstandings had held her back. Her insecurities had locked up the confessions of affection she'd longed to admit to him.

"It is not as complicated as I believed, is it? I was always trying to reason out what was happening between him and me—what drew me toward him, why I went out of my way to spend time with him whenever I could. I was afraid of the choices I'd have to make if I labeled it as love."

Annie shook her head. "You can't reason in love. If you know you love him and he loves you, too, what difference do complications make at any time, even if they do exist?"

The number of folks passing by Annie and Evelyn hadn't decreased. The wind still blew against both of their sides, playing with the edges of their dresses. The rattling roll of the wheels of buggies and carriages continued on as horses clip-clopped up and down the length of Hamilton's main road. Yet even with all the movement and sound around her, time stood still for Evelyn. All the doubt that once clouded her mind now melted away.

She stood and started back toward Blue Star. "I need to go to Breighton."

She needed to go to Jesse.

By the time she reached the ranch, the sun had settled on an evening pallor. The world was captured in a dark twilight color, and Evelyn had to draw a shawl over her shoulders as she entered the house.

She knocked on his door. No response. She strolled through the parlor. No one there. She checked every single room in the house, searching for any sign of Jesse. But he could not be found.

After completing a thorough investigation of the house, she stepped outside. Maybe he'd decided to spend the night in the bunkhouse with the other ranch hands. Or maybe he was out riding with her father, who tended to take evening rides ever since he'd recovered. He had to be somewhere around.

She turned in the direction of the bunkhouse and walked past the tree—until a small white envelope caught her eye.

Her eyes widened as she drew closer. The envelope was nestled against the back of the alcove. Honeysuckle covered the top of the letter, the dark pink petals contrasting against the starch white of the envelope. Her name covered the envelope once more—the hurried scribble Evelyn had come to love so much.

Her throat tightened. She'd written her last letter addressed to John, but if John had never written them in the first place—

After placing the honeysuckle in the pocket of her dress, she snatched up the letter and ripped open the seal. She grabbed the note out of the envelope. Her eyes scanned the page, reading over each line as if her life depended on how detailed her scrutiny was.

By the time she'd finished reading, her heart hammered in her chest. Oh, how could she have been so blind? It had been Jesse all along. It had always been him. They'd promised during that day next to the gazebo before she'd left for school. She thought they'd broken all their promises to one another.

But Jesse hadn't.

Her stomach clenched. She'd been so sure he'd given up on her. He never had. He'd kept writing and hoping, keeping up his end of the promise. He'd never, ever given up on the idea of someday being together. While the truth caved in on her chest, her heart felt like it could expand to touch the sky.

The words echoed in her mind like someone hollering in a cavern. *Can't imagine you finding a man who loves you more than I do.* She wanted to cry out for joy. She wanted to laugh at his description of John. She wanted to embrace Jesse and let him know she felt the same for him.

Still, there was no sign of him.

She scanned the ranch before her. There was no sign of any of the cowboys out in the fields. They'd all headed back to the cookhouse or the bunkhouse by now. She spotted her father's profile riding closer to the house. His horse trotted at a slow and steady pace, but Evelyn couldn't wait. She ran up to her father and his horse, clutching the letter in her hand with a tight fist.

Her father slowed his horse to a halt when he saw his daughter run toward him. Evelyn's hair flew back with a sudden gust of wind as she stopped running. Her wavy curls flew every which way as she waved the letter in the air. "Where is he, Father?"

"Who?"

"Jesse!"

Mr. Lancaster's smile at seeing her soon morphed into pressed lips and sadness in his eyes. "Jesse took off while you were gone." He jerked a thumb behind his shoulder, gesturing to the trail behind them, the trail leading far away from Breighton. "He's headed back."

Her heart sank. She felt as if someone was deflating all the hope that had swelled in her chest while reading his last letter. "No! Why would he leave?"

"Said he'd overstayed his welcome here at Breighton."

"No! No, that is not possible." She tried to deny her father's words as long as she could, but even her own stubbornness couldn't ignore the honesty in her father's tone. "Where would he go?"

"Back to California, I reckon. Said he was stopping at Raleigh for the night."

"But that is miles away!" Panic settled in her gut. She'd only been to the city once before, when she was a young girl. The trail wasn't difficult, but the journey would take hours. Wherever his final destination was, it was nowhere near Breighton.

She looked down at the letter in her hands. None of the letters had been quite as elegant as the last. But his script was the same as the other letters. There was no question Jesse was the real author of the love confessions she'd come to cherish so much.

She stared out at the trail leading away from Breighton. She hadn't felt this much loss since Jesse went away to California.

There was so much she needed to tell him! Her hand holding the letter unclenched. There was still too much he deserved to know.

Without a word to her father, Evelyn headed to the stables. She stepped into the stirrups and guided Blue Star out toward the dirt path. After one last glance at her letter, she urged the horse into a gallop across the trail. She could hear her father calling out to her to wait until morning, but she ignored him.

Pretty soon the gusts of wind muffled the sound of his voice, and the strong breeze rushed against her hair and lifted her skirts up around her ankles in a scandalous way. The cloak of night would cover her on the trail. If she kept at her pace, she hoped, she might reach Raleigh by dawn.

A wolf howled in the distance, making the hairs at the end of Evelyn's neck stand up. Yet she knew that all the wolves of Texas snapping at her heels wouldn't stop her. Images of him brushing past her in her father's study seeped into her mind.

She'd let Jesse get away once. She wouldn't make the same mistake again.

# CHAPTER TWELVE

The whiskey burned down the length of Jesse's throat. The gratifying and stinging sensation was slowly serving its purpose. He drank the last gulp from his glass, taking in the liquid as if his sanity depended on it.

His sanity really depended on how quickly he could think of something else besides the last letter he'd left at Breighton. He felt impatient for the alcohol to set in, to distract his mind from the girl he'd left behind at the ranch.

"Another?" The bartender rubbed down one of the clear glasses with a wet cloth, hoping not to lose his newest customer.

He shook his head. If he was to ride out to California as soon as possible, there was no way he could drive the wagon while drunk.

He fished out his wallet and found enough money to pay for the whiskey. Jesse placed the money on the counter and tipped his hat in the direction of the bartender. Just as he was about to get up from his seat, the bartender slapped an envelope on the counter in front of him.

"For you, sir." The bartender collected the money and left to help another customer.

He narrowed his eyes at the envelope. Maybe the bartender had the wrong fella. He hadn't told any of the other ranch hands he was stopping at Raleigh. He hadn't even told Loretta. Was it a letter from Mr. Lancaster?

He picked up the envelope and broke the seal. With reluctance, he opened the letter and unfolded it onto the wooden counter of the saloon.

Dearest love,

That is how you always signed your letters to me. That is how you signed your last letter to me.

Well, then, Jesse Greenwood, this is my one last letter to you.

I know you never broke your promise. I realize that now. But you were not the only one who honored the promises we made that day in the gazebo. I need you to know that I never broke mine either.

I never stopped loving you. I tried to convince myself I did, the same way you were terrified of admitting your feelings to me.

I kept trying to rationalize my attraction to you. I kept trying to find reasons that drew me toward you… whether it was help with ranch work, or starting a friendship. Those were just my attempts to express my love for you, the same way you wrote these letters for me.

You were right. For us, it is all or nothing. Being just friends is never going to be enough for us, just like California will never be enough for me, and a life without an open pasture will never be enough for you.

I am sorry I could not tell you earlier. Come back to Breighton with me. My heart will follow you wherever you go, but my soul belongs in Hamilton.

I love you, Jesse Greenwood. I always have, and I always will.

Yours,

Eve

His eyes scanned the bar, looking for Evelyn. He swore he could hear his heart thumping in his ears, barely believing she was here.

There was no sight of her in the saloon. He walked over to the bartender, polishing the glass at the other end of the bar. "Who gave you this letter?"

"Someone brought it in. Said he was on orders to deliver it from some lady who'd seen you walk in here."

Jesse pushed open the doors and stepped into the setting sun of Raleigh. His eyes glanced past the myriad shops and stores. A carriage approached in front of him, and the air was filled with the chatter of busy folks running errands. He looked on the other side of the road that ran through the town.

Standing across from him was Evelyn.

He ran forward, racing past the carriage horses and dodging folks whose paths he had crossed. Once he reached her side of the trail, she jumped into his arms.

Her legs crossed around his waist, and she looped her arms around his neck. His lips were on hers in an instant. He drew her closer to him, eliminating any space remaining between them. Heat filled in the lower half of his body and he pressed her hips against his.

When they finally drew up for air, Jesse set her down on the ground. He kissed her again, with tenderness this time. He'd never felt anything quite as soft as her lips, but it soon deepened into another passionate embrace as his hands settled on her hips. When they drew apart again, he could hear older folks clucking their tongues behind them and a few whispered mutters of disgust at the inappropriate display of affection. He couldn't have cared less so long as his Eve was in his arms.

"You were right, Jesse." She pecked his lips again before she continued. "John told me he only wanted to marry me for my social standing."

"What did he say?"

"I do not matter to him. My social standing and fortune do. I should have listened to you."

"He told you that?" Anger flared in Jesse's chest. How dare Cooper have the nerve to insult her?

"That is not all." She pressed her lips together into a fine line. "He lied to me. He told me all the letters were from him."

He furrowed his brow. "When did he tell you that?"

"The day I allowed him to begin courting me." She shook her head. "Foolish as I was, I believed him. I did not know who the letters actually came from. In the beginning, I hoped you had written them." She beamed at him. "Now I know you did. But that was the reason I allowed John to court me. I thought he honestly cared for me like the author of the letters did. But that was not him. It was you all along."

He kissed her again, pouring all of his love and respect for her within that kiss. She pushed him away, laughing as she did so.

"There is more I need to tell you. The other day, in the gazebo, when I walked away from you…"

He shushed her. She still looked so worried. "It doesn't matter anymore. It's okay."

"No, no, it is not." Her eyes turned to him with a softer gaze than he'd ever seen before. "I didn't want to pull away from you. I wanted more than anything to stay there, on the pasture, spending my whole day with you. That was the same reason why I left. I was just overwhelmed with all the feelings I buried in my heart for you. I assumed at that point that you did not care for me after all, and the shock of suddenly realizing that your feelings had never changed scared me."

He brushed a lock of hair behind her ear. "I never gave up on us, Evelyn. But I did keep hiding behind those letters. It's in the past now."

She shot him a bitter smile. "If there is anything I have learned from you, Jesse, it is that there is no such thing as a matter staying in the past."

"I'm just sorry I couldn't get to you earlier." He shook his head. "It took us a long time to finally reach this point."

"Do you think we wasted all this time?" The corner of her mouth quirked upward. "Imagine if I'd taken you up on that offer to run away with you that day. What if we had left Texas and Breighton and started a life for ourselves?"

Eloped, married, run away, never looked back. The idea had seemed so flawless at the age of sixteen.

Just like Loretta's threat to elope.

How angry he'd been at how she disobeyed him, how worried he'd been for her safety, how he'd nearly lost hope of finding his baby sister. He and Evelyn would have caused the same reaction around everyone else they cared about. Loretta, Mr. Lancaster, Preston—they all would have been worried sick about them.

"When you are young, you do not think about consequences. You live for yourself, ignoring your responsibilities to others." Jesse realized she had been thinking of the same possible scenario. "All we could think about was irresponsible impatience, wanting to be together right away."

"You would've never been happy." He pressed Evelyn closer to him, as if afraid someone was going to swoop in and take her away. "I don't think we wasted time. It took us this long for us to grow up enough for each other."

"There is no one else I would rather be with than you."

Courage rose in his chest. "Eve, I have enough money saved up, and I can sell my hotel in California to someone else. Breighton's your home, and it's mine, too. I can help your father run the ranch. I know I don't have a ring right now, but would you do me the honor of being my..." He began to kneel down, but she stopped him. She pulled him up to stand again, a grin on her face as she did so.

"Yes. Yes, I will." She practically bounced on her heels in excitement at first, and the eagerness of her tone left no doubt in his mind. Evelyn cradled one of his cheeks in her palm and stroked across his cheek with her thumb. The touch caused him to draw in a sharp breath. Her voice was low. "There is no one else in the world I want to marry besides you, Jesse Greenwood."

He wanted to whoop for joy. He kissed her again, crushing her lips against his. She responded to the kiss, threading her fingers through his hair as she leaned against him. When they pulled away to gasp for air, he twirled a lock of her dark hair around his finger. Her wavy hair was down and fell past her shoulders, just framing the front of her dress. The blue dress she'd worn the day of Loretta's wedding always looked so stunning on her.

He didn't think it was possible for a woman to be more gorgeous than she looked in that moment. "You're beautiful, Eve." He relished finally saying the words aloud. He didn't have to worry about her running away from him. There was no other man to court her, and there was no father to avoid. She was finally his, and he was finally hers.

Evelyn's voice was suddenly quiet. "When you left for California at first, I thought eventually I would be able to get over you. Every suitor who asked my father for permission to come calling, I turned down. One by one. I kept expecting the same feeling I felt when I was with you. But I never felt that way about any of them. Not even John. When I saw you with Annie, I thought, 'He has finally moved on. He has finally found that feeling again.'"

"Eve, I've never loved anyone else."

"I know, and I trust that now." Evelyn's voice grew firm. "You are the one I love too. I talked to Annie. She made me realize I was giving up on you, actually. But that is not going to happen." She frowned. "You know that, right? I am never going to give you up again."

Jesse pulled her toward him, wrapping her in his arms. She nestled her head in the crevice between his neck and his shoulder. "Neither am I."

He felt Evelyn's lips curve into a smile.

# EPILOGUE

The wind whipped Evelyn's hair behind her. She leaned closer to her mare, urging Blue Star further down the path. Hooves galloped behind her, closing the distance. Fear struck her heart as he began to catch up to her.

Evelyn glanced over her shoulder at the man hot on her trail. He was gaining speed, and quickly, too. Only a few yards were between them, she estimated. Evelyn turned forward again. Her house was just within sight over the rise of the pasture. *So close to safety.*

She heard the man behind her yelling as he gained speed, but she couldn't make out the exact words over the thundering of Blue Star's galloping hooves. Nothing would slow her down.

The corral posts came closer and closer, until she was nearly there. Evelyn held her breath as the man's horse came up to hers and began riding beside her. She could see him out of the corner of her eye, but didn't waste any energy looking directly at him. Instead, she urged Blue Star onward. The horse whinnied, and charged forward at the corral.

"Hurry up, Evelyn!" Preston called. He waved at her from the steps, beckoning his arms inward. She could even see Loretta standing up from the porch chair, watching the chase with wide eyes.

The man charging next to her cursed under his breath. The corral posts were just within reach. Her horse burst forward in a sudden gust of speed, and Evelyn's hand slapped the first wooden post of the corral with a cry of celebration.

She turned around. Grinning at the losing rider, she folded her arms over her chest. "Seems like the student has advanced beyond the teacher, Jesse."

After stepping off the stirrups, he walked toward her. "Almost had you that time, Eve."

"Almost, but not quite." She held Jesse's outstretched hand as she descended. As soon as her boots hit the ground, he gripped her hips and pinned her against him. She gasped.

"Think I've got you now, though," Jesse teased, smirking as he did so. Evelyn swatted his shoulder, but didn't step out of the embrace.

"Momma! Momma! I told Uncle Preston you would win!"

She turned her head in the direction of a six-year-old brown-haired boy stumbling down the steps and racing toward her. "Is that so, Ben? Seems like you know how slow Papa is." She bent down and squeezed her son's hands.

The little boy beamed at her. Then he turned to Jesse. A very solemn look crossed the child's face. "I'm very sorry you lost, Papa. I think you are getting slow."

"Slow, am I? I'll show you how slow I am." He scooped up Benjamin in his arms and threw him into the air. Benjamin laughed as he achieved weightlessness in his father's arms. Jesse caught him, and then tossed him up again.

"Again, Papa! Do it again!"

"Jesse! Stop that!" Evelyn stood up. She placed both of her hands on her hips, staring down the misbehaving men in her life. Lord forbid the day Ben slipped out of his grasp and hit his head on the ground. "Be careful."

Benjamin groaned, all advocacy for his mother lost. "Momma!"

Jesse caught Ben a final time and then set him on the ground. He put his hands on his knees to bend down and face Ben at eye level. "Seems like your Momma may be fast, but she sure doesn't know how to have any fun."

He scooped up Ben in his arms and held him against his shoulder, one arm underneath the boy and the other against his back. For all the times he threw Ben into the air (too many), whenever he held his son she knew Jesse would never let him go. Her heart swelled at the sight.

She could see the small bobbing of her son's head as he nodded at his father's words. "You need to teach her how to have fun."

"I reckon I can do that. I know a few ways your momma likes to have fun." Jesse winked at Evelyn.

Preston and Loretta walked down the porch steps and toward Evelyn. Preston stuck out his hand and congratulated her. "You're the only one who's ever been able to beat Greenwood over here. Good to take him down a peg or two before he gets too big for his britches."

"Hey!" He turned in Preston's direction and shot him a warning look. "I can still beat you in a race any day."

"Oh, but so can Evelyn," Loretta laughed. Cupping her hand and placing it over her mouth, she leaned closer next to Evelyn's ear and whispered, "The day when he's finally able to beat you in a race is the same day that hell freezes over."

"Reckon they're conspiring against us, Jesse." Preston crossed his arms and inclined his head toward Jesse's. "Quick, tell me something so it looks like we're telling secrets too."

"I want to know a secret!" Ben lifted up his head from his father's shoulder and looked around at the adults. "Someone tell me what the secret is!"

"The secret," Evelyn said, leaning closer to her son, "is that it is time for you to go to bed."

Ben scowled. "That ain't no secret, Momma." He sighed as Jesse set him down. "Do I have to go to bed?"

Jesse kneeled down next to his son and grinned. "If you go to bed now, I'll take you riding tomorrow morning."

Ben's eyes lit up with excitement. "You promise, Papa?"

"Promise. I never break any promise of mine." Jesse stood up.

One of the maids came outside and outstretched her hand toward Ben's. The child gripped the maid's hand and led her up the stairs, practically skipping over the idea of racing the next morning.

"Speaking of bedtimes, it's high time Loretta and I started heading back." Preston nodded his head in Jesse's direction. Loretta embraced both her brother and her sister-in-law before following her husband toward the buggy.

As Preston's horses rolled away toward Loretta's house, Evelyn turned to her husband and narrowed her eyes at him.

"Jesse! Ben's barely six years old. He is much too young to be riding."

He shrugged. "He's the same age I was when I learned." He always held her hand when they began to quarrel, the most ridiculous habit in the world. Still, she leaned against his shoulder as they turned back toward the house. "The boy lives on a ranch, Eve. If I don't teach him, another cowboy will."

She hated to admit her husband was right. She squeezed his hand. "All right. On one condition."

"What will that be?" Jesse opened the door for her.

She stepped inside and spun around as soon as the door closed behind him. "I teach him how to ride horses as well."

He kissed her on the lips. The kiss took her by surprise, and she pulled away. She felt as lightheaded as the time he'd kissed her when she was fifteen. "Jesse! Ben could see us. He is still awake, you know."

"Just happy you came around, that's all."

"Oh." Evelyn licked her lips as her husband stared back at her with that look of his. The look that sent a thrill down her spine and spread warmth within her heart. The look that told her she was loved. "Well, Mr. Greenwood, maybe I could take a little more convincing…"

He smirked.

"More than happy to do so, Mrs. Greenwood."

# About The Author

**Pema Donyo** is a coffee-fueled college student by day and a creative writer by night. She currently lives in sunny Southern California, where any temperature less than 70 degrees is freezing and flip-flops never go out of season. As a current student at Claremont McKenna, she's still working on mastering that delicate balance between finishing homework, meeting publisher deadlines, and—*college*. While unfortunately she's never beaten anyone in a horse race or rescued someone from a burning barn, she has put those two things on her "To Do" list. Keep in touch with her through her website at *http://pemadonyo.wordpress.com*, or her Twitter @PemaDonyo.

# A Sneak Peek from Crimson Romance
## (From *Once Upon a Wager* by Julie LeMense)

*July 1808*
*St. James Street, London*

Alec Carstairs, heir to the eighth Earl of Dorset, looked down at the letter on his desk, torn between feelings of frustration and something else he refused to acknowledge. Her handwriting was as awful as ever—undisciplined, like the young woman herself— but he knew better than to blame any long-suffering governess. Annabelle Layton did as she pleased. She always had, regardless of the consequences.

> Alec,
>
> I am sorry, as you well know. Two years is past time to forgive me, don't you think? The whole episode is best forgotten. You needn't miss Gareth's party again. I do not, I believe, have a sickness that is catching.
>
> Please say you will come.
>
> Your erstwhile friend,
>
> Annabelle Layton

A ragged sigh escaped him, the force of it sending the missive skittering across his desk, a Tudor-era monstrosity sent over from his family's London town home. Of course he'd forgiven her, if that was even the right word. She'd been so young then—just sixteen—uninhibited and free, with little thought for propriety or decorum. Forgetting the incident, however, was another matter entirely. It had irrevocably changed the way he saw her... to his everlasting shame.

"My sister insisted I hand deliver it," Gareth said, dropping himself into a tufted armchair across from the desk, startling Alec from his thoughts. He'd all but forgotten Layton's presence in the room, an unintended slight that had thankfully gone unnoticed. Alec's distraction would only have piqued Gareth's curiosity. After all, Gareth, like Annabelle, wasn't easily ignored. Both were golden haired and blue-eyed—a gift from the stunning Lady Layton. They'd been the boon companions of his otherwise lonely childhood. But none of them was a child anymore.

"Say yes, Carstairs. If you are any kind of friend, you'll not make me go back to Astley Castle by myself. God knows I'd rather stay in London."

So would Alec, but he undoubtedly had different reasons for that sentiment. "My schedule is very full, Gareth. My father has secured a new seat for me in the House of Commons, and I must memorize the current legislation. It sounds like another excuse, but it is not." And it wasn't. Not really. Alec felt the press of his new position closing in all around him: the impressive bachelor lodgings, the tailored wardrobe from Weston, the stacks of leather-bound folios packed with Parliamentary proposals. The eighth earl insisted that his son's surroundings reflect his recently elevated status.

"Have I ever told you your father frightens me? I swear his face would split down the center if he attempted a smile."

"He is stern," Alec admitted, "but only because he takes his responsibilities so seriously." As a child, he'd been frightened of his father, as well.

"Well, he is a spoilsport all the same. You're only twenty-five. Why must you bother with the Commons?"

"I'd rather talk about the party, Gareth. I should think you'd be eager to attend. It will celebrate *your* birthday, after all."

"Yes, but who knows what they've planned? Last year, the order of precedence going into dinner was decided not by titles, mind you, but by the high scores from an archery contest Annabelle organized out on the lawn.”

Alec refused to smile, despite the temptation. “Surely she didn’t lead the way into dinner? She hasn’t even made her debut.” To do so would have been highly improper. But not atypical.

“How did you know Annabelle won?”

“Of course she did. You’re forgetting we taught her the finer points of the game.” Just as they’d taught her to shoot pistols, bet on cards, and ride bareback. He’d had a hand, he supposed, in making her into the hoyden she’d become.

“Annabelle will always play to her interests,” Gareth admitted. “Which means that this year, there will be lots of dancing at the party. She’s mad for it, all of that spinning and skipping about. I ask you, who wants a Scottish reel back home when I can dance with the high-flyers in Covent Garden? Now there’s a dance I don’t mind doing.”

An inappropriate image of Annabelle came to mind, but Alec forced it aside, turning his focus on her brother. “You look as colorful as any bird-of-paradise in the Garden, Gareth. That satin waistcoat is nearly blinding in the afternoon light. My eyesight may not recover.”

“Just because Brummell dresses like an undertaker doesn’t mean that I have to be similarly sepulchral. Especially when there is a party I must attend. Say you will come. I don’t know the reason behind your estrangement with Annabelle—and do not deny there is one—but I’m certain that she’s to blame. She can be a maddening creature. Still, she misses your friendship. She said… let me think… that it ‘had more value than you have lately accorded it.’ I had to promise to say exactly those words.”

Ah, their friendship. Old and inviolable once. Annabelle’s barbs, like her arrows, were always well aimed.

With a deep breath, and before he could stop himself, Alec took a sheet of parchment and scribbled a few words upon it. He then folded it upon itself. He extracted a stick of sealing wax from a side drawer, heating it briefly above the beeswax oil lamp on his desk. He dripped a small puddle of wax where the folds met, and pressed it with his signet ring. Satisfied the seal would hold fast against Gareth's attempts to loosen it, Alec handed him the note. "I will be there," he said. "But I have little doubt I will regret it."

Gareth merely chuckled. "If you're going to regret something, make the pain of it worthwhile. Come join me at The Anchor on Park Street. I plan on getting well and truly drunk before I meet up with Digby to play cards. It will lessen the sting of my certain defeat."

"Damien Digby is an ass. He makes you risk too much."

"I can only stand one respectable friend, Alec. And that would be you," Gareth added, "in case you're wondering."

"You say 'respectable' instead of 'boring' to spare my feelings, I know. Go on without me. If I'm to travel to Nuneaton for your birthday, there are things I must do." Like memorizing names, organizing arguments, and—above all else—practicing a brotherly smile.

After Gareth departed, Alec pushed away from his desk, and walked over to the study's large bay window, which looked out upon St. James Street below. Bracing his hands against the sun-warmed panes, he watched carriages and pedestrians move down the cobble-stoned thoroughfare, regretting his impulsiveness. Undoubtedly, his decision was a poor one. What would Annabelle read into his reply?

Annabelle,

I've missed our friendship, too. I will see you at Gareth's party. But you must promise to keep your clothes on.

As he waited for his father to join him in the library at Dorset House, Alec took a brief glance at its worn leather tomes, all lined up in an orderly fashion along dozens of age-darkened wood shelves. This was Henry Carstairs's domain, the inner sanctum where he built his political coalitions, and entertained allies with brandy after dinner. On the rare occasions Alec had been in London as a child, it had also been the room where Father meted out his punishments. Perhaps that was why Edmunds, their butler, had seated him here, rather than in the family drawing room. The earl's note had hinted at his strong displeasure, though Alec was long past the age of birch rods and bloodied hands.

As if summoned by his thoughts, the earl strode into the room, a sheaf of papers tucked under his arm, his reading spectacles perched on the edge of his nose, making his eyes seem owlish. Trim and fighting-fit, Father would make for a very intimidating owl indeed, though Alec now bested him in height by two inches. He was no longer the small, sickly boy who had so often been ignored, along with his mother. He'd finally earned his father's attention, even his respect, despite their high price. Standing quickly, he offered a quick bow. "Good morning, Father. You wished to see me."

"Take your seat," the earl said, settling into the large baronial chair behind his desk. "I was not happy to learn that you are going to Nuneaton for the Layton boy's fete, when you should be here preparing for the Commons."

"Even allowing for travel there and back, I will only be gone three days. I'll be bringing along the summaries prepared for me, and I've memorized the names of all the members, as well as their political positions."

His father shifted in the chair, displeasure obvious in the tight set of his jaw. "I expected you to join us for dinner tomorrow.

Lord Fitzsimmons and his daughter, Jane, will be in attendance. He's proven a useful ally in Parliament, and the girl is a reliable and sober sort. She'd make a good wife for you."

Of late, Father had mentioned marriage repeatedly, and Miss Fitzsimmons in particular. "I'm sorry I was not informed of your plans," Alec replied. "I cannot attend. I've already accepted the invitation to Astley Castle."

"To travel there for a such a short trip, when our Arbury Hall will have to be readied. I think it an imposition."

The Hall, which bordered the Layton estate, was kept in a constant state of readiness, because Father expected nothing less. It wouldn't be wise, though, to point that out. "I won't be staying at the Hall. I'll stop by to have the carriage checked and to greet the servants, but I will sleep at the castle. They'll have a number of overnight guests."

"Those guests won't be from the best families, I can assure you. And the Layton boy is drinking and gambling himself into the grave. I don't like that you associate with him."

"I don't share his vices, Father."

"No, but never underestimate the allure of recklessness. The boy is shockingly irresponsible, and the girl is at an age now when your childhood friendship might be mistaken for something more."

"I am well aware of that."

"Annabelle Layton is the sort that invites scandal. The whole family is, which is something we can't afford, not if all my plans for you are to be realized."

"They are good people who mean no harm."

"They are remarkably odd. Lady Charlotte is weak-minded, and Sir Frederick… I've rarely met a more compulsive man. Nervous and awkward, but mention some sort of flying insect, and he'll prattle on for hours. Lepidopterology is all the rage, but I can't abide butterflies."

When Alec was a child, quiet in a lonely household, the Laytons had seemed exuberant, exotic even. They'd lived and loved with abandon, while he and his own mother had been starved of affection. Alec couldn't fight back a flash of anger at the memory. But those days were past. With hard work and dedication, he'd found a way to earn his father's love. And not just for himself.

But it was true that Gareth was increasingly a victim of his weaknesses. Just yesterday, he'd tried to talk Alec into a large wager. Lord Chetwiggin's grays were racing against Lord Sherford's blacks in a torchlit sprint on Hampstead Heath. Alec and Gareth would leave for Nuneaton beforehand, but Digby was placing a bet in Gareth's stead. Undoubtedly, it would be made for far more than he could afford.

"I'll not return with a passion for lepidopterology, Father. I can withstand a brief exposure to their family." And to Annabelle.

Those owlish eyes were fixed upon him, their expression severe.

"You mean to disagree with me on this?"

"Shall I break my word, then? That is not the man you've raised me to be. This will be a party in the country with old friends, and nothing more."

The room was ominously quiet.

"If you must go, then go," his father said at last. "But remember who you are, and what I expect. Don't do anything that will have unfortunate repercussions. And stay away from Annabelle Layton."

•••

Annabelle was thrilled to see the familiar handwriting on the back of her note, but she was less thrilled reading it. In fact, only the most rigid self-control kept her from stomping one of her darling green half boots on the stone floor of the terrace. Could he not be done with it? Did he not remember the heat of that morning? The very air had simmered, like a pot set to boil. She'd been unable to sleep. Astley Castle's fountain, hidden from view in the formal gardens, had beckoned like the wellspring of salvation.

She'd known full well that her behavior was scandalous. Ladies did not swim in fountains after all, but the water had felt so wonderful. And she *had* been wearing clothes: a linen shift, even though the water made it rather revealing. Certainly, she'd not expected Alec to be out wandering the castle grounds at dawn, a witness to her shameless display. He had gone utterly still at the sight of her, like a pillar of salt caught between Sodom and Gomorrah.

Even now, she could remember his eyes. Something had burned in them, and she'd hoped, despite her embarrassment, that he'd finally understood she was no longer a child. That she could be more to him than a friend. But the past two years had laid waste to those notions. The only thing burning that day had been his indignation.

Later—after she'd been trussed back up in a suffocating corset and a long-sleeved gown—he'd warned her about the dangers a young woman could face, sounding just like Parson Withersby at a Sunday service. Not that the parson had ever been so breathtakingly handsome.

Since then, however, Alec had come up with an astonishing array of excuses to avoid her. The amusing letters they'd once exchanged with great regularity were now limited, on his part, to polite inquiries about her well being. He was too busy in London being molded into the man his father thought he should be. A man who was hidebound and self-important.

Startled from her pique by the sound of laughter, Annabelle leaned over the terrace balustrade, looking out onto the back lawn. Her parents were chasing butterflies—her mother's hair unbound and floating behind her, her father's shirttails flying like flags in the breeze, both of them swinging their nets with wild abandon. Their plan was to catch dozens of the colorful insects, so they could be released in the Great Hall during Gareth's party. However, she'd have to speak with Mother about that. Those plans had to be changed. Annabelle wanted this party to be remembered for its decorum. If only to shock Alec.

•••

"Gareth, that is the largest trunk I've ever seen," she said the next morning as her brother burst into the hall in blur of color. "I hope it means you will be staying for a while. It would do both you and your purse some good."

"I can't be poorly dressed at my own birthday party," Gareth said, wrapping her in a quick hug after instructing the footmen to take his belongings to his room. He was wearing a bright green jacket over a puce-striped vest and fawn trousers—obviously a statement of high, if unfortunate, style. "Besides, there's nothing wrong with my purse. I've had a rush of luck at the tables lately, and I'm expecting to hear the news of my biggest win yet once Digby arrives."

"Who is this Digby? You've not mentioned him before."

"Damien Digby. I met him a few months back. He has got a gift for picking winners. I think you'll like him."

She doubted it. She didn't like anyone who indulged her brother's gambling habit. He regularly exceeded his allowance. Whenever he came home from London, he and Father closeted themselves in the study, arguing about money in angry whispers.

Of course, he invariably returned to the city with an additional bank draft. Her parents liked to joke that Gareth could charm the stripes off the famous zebra at Astley's Amphitheater. With a ready smile, he was so undeniably good-looking that most of her friends were madly in love with him. He got whatever he wanted. They both did.

176

Which is what made the matter of Alec Carstairs so infuriating.

"You shouldn't be spending so much of Father's money, Gareth. Have you forgotten that I'll be going to London for the Little Season in September?"

"How could I? You prattle on about it in every letter. I've warned all of my friends. We're going to decamp en masse to Brighton."

"I will ignore your insults," she said, fighting back a grin. "Tell me, what does Alec think about this Mr. Digby?"

"You can guess the answer to that, Annabelle. Honestly, Carstairs has forgotten how to have fun. Any day now, I expect to find he's gone old and arthritic."

Even so, he was still the most handsome man she'd ever seen. And tonight, she would not be ignored. Mrs. Markum from the village had made up the most beautiful dress for her. It was the palest of cream silks, shot through with silver thread, and delicately embroidered with tiny flowers. Her hair would be pulled back with the clips Father had given to Mother on their wedding day. They were shaped like butterflies, the wings sparkling with dozens of small diamonds.

Tonight, she would dare him to find a trace of the girl he pretended her to be.

• • •

Just as evening fell, Alec walked up the crushed stone drive to Astley Castle. Despite its rather grandiose name, it was more accurately a fortified manor house, although it did have a moat. Briefly the home of Lady Jane Grey, England's unfortunate Nine Days Queen, it had also served as a garrison for Cromwell's forces during the Civil War before passing into the Layton family. Tonight, however, the house gave no hint of its troubled history. Japanese lanterns were strung, not only in the trees leading up the drive, but also in those surrounding the house, and the effect was magical. In the early dusk, a gentle light bathed the grounds, softening the lines of the old home, coloring it with pale pinks and darker purples. Alec heard strains of music and conversation. In fact, it appeared to be a remarkably conventional party, which was something of a surprise. Surely, circus animals were lurking somewhere.

The oversized front door was open to the evening air, and dozens of people were assembled in the Great Hall, which was brightly lit with wall lanterns. Chandeliers decked with wax candles flickered high above as Gareth's parents received their guests. Sir Frederick, who often panicked in crowds, was hiding his misgivings well, and Lady Layton was radiant beside him. Gareth stood next to her, dressed in a colorful approximation of evening attire, but he seemed distracted. His eyes were darting the crowd and looking for someone. A footman with the champagne tray, no doubt. Alec did not see Annabelle.

But then familiar, melodious laughter washed over him, and he turned. A willowy, honey-tressed blonde stood at the center of a crowd of adoring men. Her face was hidden from view, but her gown—the color of moonlight—caressed her curves like a lover. Alec braced himself, every nerve taut. As if sensing his presence, she looked over her shoulder and smiled.

God in Heaven, he should never have come here tonight.

Annabelle had been only four years old the first time he saw her. He'd joined his mother on a neighborly visit to Astley Castle, and the little girl had utterly charmed him, struggling to sit still while Lady Layton served tea to her guests. Delicate, soft, and pink, like a rosy-cheeked doll, she'd roused all his protective instincts before kicking him in the shins to gain his attention.

If only he could see the girl she'd once been in the woman standing before him. Even two years ago, there had been hints of her, hiding in the body of a goddess. But there was nothing childlike about Annabelle now. She was spectacularly lovely, with arched brows, high cheekbones, and cornflower blue eyes that took his breath away.

Excusing herself from her admirers, she walked toward him with a slow smile. Then again, walking was not the right word. Swaying was the better choice, and all he could do was stand there, heart slamming in his chest as she approached, the gossamer silk gown caressing her curves. Were it dampened—as was the fashion with London's faster set—it would be almost transparent. Just like that morning when she had gone swimming in the fountain, casting a spell over him like a sorceress.

"Alec, how nice you could join us this evening. I worried that in the end, something pressing would keep you in London. So often in these past two years, that has been the case." Once, she'd have embraced him impulsively, laughing all the while. Now, she gave a surprisingly ladylike curtsey, extending one gloved hand. He leaned down to press a kiss upon it, and if his lips lingered a moment too long, he was rather proud of his self-control. It had been just enough to breathe in the scent of her—a familiar mix of honeysuckle soap and the lemon drops she loved. But there was also something new. Something dangerous.

"I wrote that I would be here, Annabelle. I am man who honors my obligations."

She tilted her head, angling it up toward him, her eyes bewitching beneath half-lowered lashes. "Is that what I am now? An obligation?"

She would scramble his wits if he wasn't careful.

"Of course not. We're old friends, despite the distance between us."

He'd been referring to the distance between London and Nuneaton, but he was certain she had leaned closer. His body all but screamed it.

"Perhaps we can ease that distance tonight."

God above. Did she have any idea how that might be interpreted? He managed a self-conscious pat on her shoulder before stepping back, hoping he appeared collected and calm, instead of dizzy with the nearness of her.

"You are looking very well," he said after a long pause. "How… big you have become."

And with that asinine statement, he turned on his heels, vanishing into the crowd.

• • •

Why must Alec be indifferent to her, when so many other men were eager to gain her attention? There was Horace Briarly, the squire's son from the village. He'd vowed his eternal love these past three years or more. Lord Percival Spencer, the rather rakish heir to a viscountcy in Warwickshire, made every excuse to visit her father with lepidopterological concerns—though it was obvious he had no interest in the hobby. And then there was the widower, Sir Boniface, an amateur artist. He'd already presented her with a number of lovely paintings, although it was embarrassing to have six portraits of oneself. Wherever Annabelle went, men seemed to sprout up like spring flowers.

But none of them was as endlessly *fascinating* as Alec Carstairs. So noble and decent. So restrained and responsible. The one reliable constant of her childhood, he'd become the man against whom she measured all others.

Not to mention the beauty of him. Wide shoulders, narrow hips, and long legs, all encased in immaculately tailored clothing. Dark brown hair, still wavy but shorter now than she remembered. Beautiful lips, wide and generous. Prominent cheekbones and a straight nose that flared slightly. Those toffee-colored eyes that always reminded her of Cook's caramels, still warm from the stove.

Gaining his attention this evening required a new strategy. But she couldn't plot effectively if she was caught up in a conversation with Horace, who was heading her way like a hound on a scent. She quickly blessed the wall of potted palms beside the door. With a quick movement, she slipped behind them, escaping out onto the drive.

As escapes went, it was poorly planned. It was a party, after all. Guests were getting out of their carriages and walking up the meandering stone pathway to the castle entrance. Distracted by thoughts of Alec, she walked directly into a small group of men who were newly arrived. One of them caught her with his arms, steadying her before she could knock both of them down. Glancing up at the blunt-featured man, she offered a hasty apology and spun away. He called after her, but she was in no mood to speak with strangers. She headed into the castle's elaborate gardens and the swiftly descending darkness.

Passing clipped boxwoods and yews set in a pattern dating to Elizabethan times, she followed a gravel path into the heart of the gardens where a Roman folly stood, reflected in a semicircular ornamental pond, her fountain at its center. The pond was filled with gold and silver fish, and as a child, she'd loved watching sunlight shimmer on their scales through the water. Several bubbled to the surface at her approach, hopeful and expectant, but tonight, she had nothing to offer but a half smile.

There was a bench hidden behind the folly, and she took a seat there. Her collision had wreaked havoc with the elaborate coiffure her maid, Mary, had created. Annabelle fumbled with an errant clip, but that sent another wave of heavy hair tumbling over her shoulders. It wouldn't do to be seen in this state. She could only imagine what Alec would think. At least, the new Alec. The one who was so stuffy. Thankfully, though, she was alone.

Until quite suddenly, she was not.

"I was sure my eyes had deceived me, but they did not. You are exquisite."

The voice belonged to a strange man, his approach almost silent in the soft grass. Annabelle merely edged further into the shadows. "Sir, I don't wish to be rude, but I would prefer to be alone."

"But your beauty holds me spellbound," he said easily, as if he'd practiced the line.

She looked up. It was the blunt-featured man. He had light brown hair and pale gray eyes, and while she could not guess at his age, he was far older than she. "This is hardly the time for false flattery. And the party is that way." She pointed needlessly toward the house.

He moved slowly toward her. "What is your name?"

"As you well know, it would hardly be proper for me to say. We've not been introduced." Nor should she be alone with him here in the dark.

"Such becoming modesty." He smiled, flashing uneven teeth. "But I insist on knowing who you are." He took another step closer as he slowly withdrew the glove covering his left hand. "Tell me, my dear, if I trailed my fingers down your cheek, would your skin be as soft as it appears?"

So he was that sort of man. "You should know that I always carry a small pistol on my person," she said, her voice impressively calm. "Just in case an unfortunate situation like this one should arise."

"Really?" His eyes gleamed in the darkness. "Why don't I feel my hands along your body, and see if I can discover the place where you've hidden it?"

"Touch her," another voice ground out, "and I will break both of your arms."

Alec. He'd followed her, after all. He was suddenly towering over the stranger.

"Carstairs, what an unpleasant surprise. The lady and I are having a private discussion."

Ignoring him, Alec turned to face her. "Are you all right?" Taking in her disheveled appearance, he added tersely, "Has he hurt you in any way?"

"No, I am fine," Annabelle replied, masking her relief. "I merely needed some fresh air."

"I meant no harm," the man said, raising his hands in mock surrender. "I was merely engaging in an innocent flirtation with a desirable woman."

"She's little more than a child," Alec bit out. And as offended as she was by his comment, this didn't seem like a time to argue.

"She is hardly a child, Carstairs," the man drawled. "If she were, I doubt you'd be treating me to such a manly display."

She could sense the tension in Alec. He was keeping his temper in check, but just barely.

"Who are you?" Annabelle asked. "Why are you here in my home?"

"Your home?" His eyes widened with surprise. "You must be Miss Layton, Gareth's sister. He and I are very close friends."

"Of late," she said, "he has been less particular in his friendships."

The stranger darkened at that. "As it turns out, we are business partners of a sort. I am Damien Digby, at your service."

Gareth had been wrong. She could not like Mr. Digby.

"How utterly perfect you are, Miss Layton. When your brother spoke of your beauty, I thought he exaggerated. I can see now he was being coy. I will look forward to seeing you inside."

With a cold look at Alec, he turned and strode purposefully toward the house.

• • •

"Don't you know enough not to run off without a proper escort, Annabelle?" Alec demanded, anger sharpening his voice.

At his tone, her own temper flared. "I was more than fine, Alec. I've grown… what was the word you used? Oh yes, big. I'm big now, like a sturdy tree out in the lawn. Perhaps if you think on it, you can come up with an even more unflattering term. In the meantime, I will take care of myself."

"Don't be foolish. You don't know what a man like that is capable of."

"You heard him say he meant no harm." Even as she spoke the words, she knew they were false. She'd seen the look in Digby's eyes.

"He is a cad, the very worst sort." Alec put a hand to the edge of his cravat, as if it were suddenly too tight. "And much as it pains me to say so, you are at an age when such men will seek you out."

"I cannot help the fact that I've grown up, Alec. I'm sorry the end result of it has been so unfortunate."

He met that statement with a long moment of silence, merely watching her in the moonlight, a muscle twitching in his jaw. "I don't think that is the right word."

She didn't want to find out which word he would choose instead. Her confidence had been battered enough for one evening. "I have to return to the party." She started to move away, but he put his hands on her shoulders to still her.

"Have you really taken to carrying around pistols, Annabelle?"

"Of course not. I was bluffing. I would never ruin the line of this lovely dress."

His eyes sparked briefly with amusement, and perhaps admiration. "Lovely as your dress is, you can't return to the party looking as you do. Let me help you."

He reached down to loosen one of the diamond clips tangled in her hair, and slowly worked it free, standing so close she had to remind herself to breathe. He smelled of sandalwood and crisp, clean linen. "This one will also have to be reset," he said, moving to the other clip, his amusement fading. In moments, the rest of her hair tumbled down to her waist, and he ran his fingers through its long length in an effort to smooth it. Then he cleared his throat, dropping his hands to his sides.

"I'm not much of a lady's maid." He tucked the clips into her gloved hands and stepped back.

"People will wonder what we've been doing out here in the dark," she said, daring him to think of her that way. But his face was inscrutable, and she fought back a stab of frustration. "Of course, no one would suspect you of misbehaving. You are far too honorable. You're practically my brother."

"I am not your brother, Annabelle. And I'm not as honorable as you think." Abruptly, he turned toward the castle. "Follow me to the servants' entrance, and go up to your room from there." She hurried to keep up with his long strides. "Go straight to your maid," he called over his shoulder. "Dinner will be served soon. Your absence will be noticed if you don't hurry."

He was dismissing her, because she was a foolish girl he neither wanted nor needed. It was evident in every terse, clipped word.

When they reached the house, she passed quietly through the doorway leading into the kitchen. In the confusion, as the staff prepared trays of food to be brought up for dinner, she was able to slip by unnoticed. In moments, she was up the stairs.

. . .

Only when she'd vanished from sight did Alec allow his careful control to slip. The ghosts of his past were all around him. He and Gareth and Annabelle, rolling down the hillside over there on that warm spring day, laughing aloud as governesses and tutors ran after them, bemoaning grass stains and inappropriate behavior. That long ago summer night, sitting with Annabelle on the bench behind the folly, her hand in his, because while she loved to look up at the stars, she was frightened of the dark. That afternoon when he'd come down from Oxford for a visit, and she leapt into his arms. His only searing thought had been, "how beautiful you've become." That morning two years ago, when everything changed.

He hadn't been able to sleep. It had been intensely hot, even at that early hour of the morning, so he'd gone for a walk, hoping for a breeze. Hearing her laughter, he'd been drawn to it, never expecting to find Annabelle dancing in the fountain, a pagan goddess of the dawn, water coursing over every nearly naked curve. The pink tips of her breasts had been visible through her wet shift, and he'd felt like the worst sort of lecher for wanting her. Even now, he hardened at the memory, his mouth dry as dust.

Annabelle was free in a way he'd never been, full of life and laughter. She was warm, vital, and sparkling, like flames in the night. But never had someone been more unsuited to the path that he must follow. His happiness was not his own. It did not matter that he wanted her, that he could no longer deny his desire. How shocked she'd be to know that while he had been untangling her hair, he'd been imagining it wound around him, her body naked beneath his own.

In the mood for more Crimson Romance?
Check out *Mischief and Magnolias*
by Marie Patrick at *CrimsonRomance.com*.